M000206936

# SO WE LIE

EVA RAE THOMAS MYSTERY - PREQUEL

# WILLOW ROSE

"The fact is, lying is a necessity. We lie to ourselves because the truth, the truth freaking hurts. No matter how hard we try to ignore or deny it, eventually, the lies fall away, whether we like it or not. But here's the truth about the truth: It hurts. So we lie."

- **From *Grey's Anatomy***

# Prologue
## WASHINGTON, D.C.

They only ever fought when they were drunk. Mindy Lynn and Tuck Bowman had been together for a little more than seven years now and were known among their friends as the stable couple, the ones who never fought, who agreed on almost everything. And that was the truth, at least for the most part—until they both had a little more than they should to drink. Then it took nothing to set both of them off, and as they were driving home from the Grillfish, where they had been drinking at the bar for hours after finishing dinner, they were at each other's throats.

"Don't give me that," Tuck said, accelerating to rush through a yellow light. "I saw how you looked at him when he came over to you."

Mindy threw out her arms. "I don't even know who you're talking about, for crying out loud."

Tuck turned his head and stared at her, his blue eyes growing narrow and angry. Mindy worried that he wasn't looking at the road ahead.

"Do you love me?"

"Please, keep your eyes on the road," she said, placing her hands nervously on the glove compartment.

"I'll darn well keep my eyes where I want them," he hissed, then glared briefly ahead of them before looking at her again. He clasped her thigh hard. Pain shot through her body. Tuck had never laid a hand on her like that before. His eyes were glossy, staring blankly at her, his lips growing into a tight line. Mindy felt dizzy. She really shouldn't have taken those last two shots. She could still taste the tequila and would be so sick tomorrow. It was her problem. When they reached a certain level of drunkenness, it was like she couldn't stop. She wanted more and more. It wasn't often she allowed herself to go this far, and typically, she would have stopped a lot earlier before she reached that point of no return. But since Tuck got laid off from his construction job, things hadn't been good. They had struggled financially, and Tuck had found it hard not to be able to provide as he ought to. Not that they had any children yet, but they wanted to. They had been trying for years and struggling to face the fact that the pregnancy hadn't happened yet. Mindy often talked about seeing someone—a professional—about it but hadn't dared to mention it to Tuck yet. If something was wrong with him, it would break his heart. It would simply crush him.

"It'll come. You just need to give it time," her mom had said. "Who knows? Maybe you're worrying too much about it. It'll come when you least expect it. Heaven knows you were a huge surprise to your father and me. It's easier when you don't have any expectations."

So that's what Mindy tried not to have. Expectations. It was harder said than done, for sure. After three years of trying, it was getting difficult to ignore the facts. And tonight, she had brought it up, stupid as she was, over the fried fish platter, the same dish she always ordered in that place.

"It's been three years, Tuck. Do you think maybe something is off?"

Those were her words. That was all she had said. But it was enough. Tuck's eyes grew distant, and he barely blinked.

Before she could say anything else, he had downed his beer and asked for another one, which he drank without speaking a word to her. Mindy had cursed herself for bringing it up. It was supposed to have been a night of celebration for them because Tuck had finally landed a new job—one that paid well for once. They had been so happy up until that moment when she asked that dimwitted silly question when there was no reason to. Why did she have to ruin everything?

He had taken the drinking to the bar, and she had followed him, trying to put him in a better mood. After a couple of shots, he had finally eased up on her, and they had talked normally again. It wasn't until they made it to the car that the fighting began. Now, Tuck was accusing her of flirting with some guy she didn't even remember talking to. As always, they were avoiding what was really bothering them. They kept fighting as he turned onto Wisconsin Avenue, the car swerving on the road.

"I can't believe you," he said. "But I guess you don't love me anymore. If you loved me, you wouldn't cheat on me."

Mindy scoffed. "Cheat on you? Where is this coming from?"

"Oh, come on. How stupid do you think I am?" Tuck yelled, tapping a finger on his temple. "I know you. You've been acting so strange lately, and the other day you wouldn't let me look at your phone. You don't think I notice the signs, huh? But this is so typically you. You…"

"Please, keep your eyes on the road, Tuck!" Mindy yelled as a truck came rushing toward them, blaring its horn, blinking its headlights. Tuck pulled the wheel and turned away from it just in time. Mindy clasped her chest and breathed heavily as the truck blasted by them.

"There it is again," he said, looking at her angrily. "You thought I'd hit that truck, didn't you? You don't trust me."

That was the worst thing in Tuck's eyes—when Mindy didn't trust him to protect her. He always pulled that card when he was drunk. He would gather episodes in his mind and then rattle them off when he'd had too much. Starting with the time she asked him about the letters from the IRS that kept coming in the mail. Mindy closed her eyes with a sigh. Her head was spinning, and she felt a headache approaching behind her eyes.

"Of course, I trust you, Tuck," she lied, trying to calm him down, to make him feel better. She had done that a lot these past few years when he got like this. It usually worked, but she wasn't sure it would this time. "I was just scared. You know how nervous I get when driving after...."

Mindy trailed off when thinking about her best friend, Amy. She had been in a car crash when they were still in high school, and a car slammed head-on into hers. She had been killed on the spot.

Mindy looked out the front as a set of headlights hit them and almost blinded her.

"That car is coming toward us really fast," she said, her voice trembling.

Tuck turned to look and saw the car rushing toward them, swerving from side to side. "Oh sh...." Tuck said, turning the wheel abruptly as the car whooshed by them.

"Whoa!" Mindy exclaimed, and they both looked in the rearview mirror, following its path as it continued, then crashed into a tree on the side of the road.

# Part I

## SIX YEARS LATER

# Chapter 1

I paused for a second as I showed the uniformed woman behind the glass my badge. It was still so shiny that it was hard to hide how new it was.

"Eva Rae Wilson? Agent Wilson?"

Her eyes lifted and met mine through the glass. The sound of my name made me wince slightly. After being married five years and changing my maiden name—Thomas—out with Wilson, I still hadn't gotten used to being called that. I had discussed it intensely with my husband, Chad. I had wanted to keep Thomas because I loved that name, but he got very offended that I didn't want to carry his name, so in the end, I caved. I just liked the sound of Agent Thomas better than Agent Wilson. Don't ask me why. I guess I wasn't prepared for losing my identity like that. In my mind, I was still Eva Rae Thomas as I had been my entire life.

"I don't think I've met you before. You new?"

I nodded, blushing slightly. "Yes. Got with the bureau just recently."

She gave me an annoyed look, then lifted her eyebrows. "And you're here to see Frank Woods?"

"Yes. I've filled out all the paperwork."

7

"Okay, looking fine..." she said, looking at the papers I had handed her when arriving. "You got the signature there, and on the back as well... and your initials on page three, yes. I guess you're good to go."

She leaned over and pressed the button to open the locks on the double doors leading inside the prison. This bunker-like building only housed the worst of the criminals in the D.C. area. It was my first time there, and I wasn't without jitters. I walked through and showed my badge once again, just lifting it so the guard could see it. I enjoyed showing it still, as it was something I had worked really hard to achieve. Becoming an FBI profiler with the BAU, Behavioral Analysis Unit, was a lifelong dream of mine, and it had finally come true. I had taken four years of psychology in college, then gone through training at the FBI Academy before being stationed at a field office in D.C. for three years before applying for the BAU. I couldn't believe that I had been selected for training, and after two and a half years, I was a fully functioning FBI profiler. Now, it was time for me to show them my skills. And I knew exactly how to impress them all. The solution was standing right in front of me a few seconds later when I sat down in the interview room, and the door was opened.

"Frank Woods," I said to the guy in the orange jumpsuit. His hands and feet were chained together as he was guided inside, flanked by two guards with stern looks on their faces. He wasn't as handsome as in the pictures I had in my file in front of me, but he was still a good-looking guy. The salt and pepper on the sides of his hair suited him, and it was clear he had spent the last six years on the inside working out. He was a lot more muscular now than he had been when convicted for murdering his wife.

I pointed at the chair in front of me, smiling politely, trying my best to hide just how nervous I was.

"Have a seat. You and I have a lot to talk about."

## Chapter 2

**T**HEN:
Online dating was more challenging than she had expected it to be. Mary Ellen Garton scrolled through yet another profile on MillionairesMatch.com. She could hear her sister Frances' voice in the back of her head, telling her it was a scam, that there were not actually millionaires on this dating site.

"I mean, if you were really a millionaire, why would you need to look for a date on a website? All you'd get would be gold diggers."

Mary Ellen disagreed. It was true that most of the guys who had written to her had turned out not to be worth her time, but at some point, she was certain she would find Mr. Right. It wasn't that he needed to be a millionaire; it would just be a nice addition—like a bonus. Even though Mary Ellen was a single mom with four children, she wasn't exactly struggling. She was doing okay for herself and had taken care of them by herself for three years now while climbing the career ladder at her company. She was actually quite the businesswoman herself, and money was tight some months, but not severely. And she had finally been able to buy the house she had rented for the past five years, and with the house skyrocketing in value this past year, she had learned she now had a positive net worth.

Yes, Mary Ellen could take care of herself and her children just fine, even though her sister never believed she could. There was a lot more to Mary Ellen than her sister gave her credit for.

"I'll find the perfect match, and you'll be so jealous, Frances," while eating your own words," she mumbled to herself, scrolling through the profiles, looking at the pictures. Mary Ellen paused at one, then clicked the profile. This guy's photo showed him playing golf in those awful pants they always wore. He had a cute face, but she couldn't really deal with the fact that he was a golfer. That usually took up a lot of a man's time, and she would never see him when he was off work. That could be both good and bad. It was good to have time apart—to miss one another and not rub elbows all the time, but then again, she'd end up sitting alone with the kids all weekend and have to drive them alone to all their activities while grumbling about him being on the golf course, again. Mary Ellen's friend Jennifer had that problem with her husband, and it drove her nuts. Nope, there was no way she was going down that road. Mary Ellen shook her head, then deleted this guy's request to connect. She wasn't taking any chances. This time, the guy had to be absolutely perfect for her. And she just knew he would be. He was there some-where, waiting for her to find him. She knew it in her soul.

"Where are you, my future husband?" she said with an expec-tant smile as she scrolled further down, looking at pictures, discarding the men one after another. "I know you're in here somewhere."

She sighed as she looked at a guy she liked but then realized that he lived in France. She wasn't up for a long-distance relationship. Not that he needed to live in her backyard or even in the same county. She didn't mind driving a few hours, but she couldn't do a whole other country. She simply didn't want to.

"Nope," she said and left his profile, slightly sad that he wasn't the one since she really liked his deep blue eyes.

"It's gotta be just right. And I know it will be once I...."

Mary Ellen paused when seeing the picture of a man who had

already requested to connect with her. She stared at the picture, then took a deep breath and clicked his profile, expecting to find something wrong at first glance, as she had done with the rest of them. But to her surprise, it didn't happen this time. This guy lived only three hours away, and he was about the same age as Mary Ellen, older by two years, which was perfect. He had no children and hadn't been married before, only been in a long-term relationship with a woman who didn't want to get married. They split because of *different interests*.

And he was actually a millionaire. He wrote that he had his own house with a pool and had made money on investments that made it possible for him to retire last year at the age of only forty-eight.

*This means I will have plenty of time for a new partner in my life. And I will do my utmost to keep you happy.*

Mary Ellen stared at the picture of him standing by a willow tree, leaning against it in his black jeans and blue shirt, smiling handsomely.

She leaned back in the chair, sighing comfortably, feeling a few butterflies appear in her stomach.

"There you are, Mr. Perfect. I was wondering when you'd show up."

## Chapter 3

"Let me get this straight. You want to reopen my case?"

Frank Woods looked at me from behind his bangs that had grown long and fell into his eyes. Being in his mid-fifties, he was almost twenty-five years older than me, yet I couldn't help but find him attractive. His smile and his eyes bore a secret in them that drew me in. He had been described as a womanizer and a player in the media, but that wasn't what I saw. He was charming, yes, but not in a bad way. He wasn't flirting with me, and sitting across from him didn't make me feel as uncomfortable as I had expected. The media had painted an ugly picture of him back then, and I was beginning to think it was quite unfair.

He leaned forward, and his chains rattled.

"Do you mind elaborating?"

I smiled. "I understand why you're confused."

He scoffed. "Confused is quite the understatement. Do you have anything to base this request on? I've admitted to killing her. What can you possibly have that will prove I didn't?"

I looked down at my file, then shook my head before lifting my gaze again. "I don't have anything solid, and that's why I came to you first. I need you to give me access to your wife's things. I think they might have missed something important when going through it all six years ago, but I can't prove it. I assume you still have all your old stuff from the house? Maybe in boxes somewhere?"

He cleared his throat. "Well, my sister-in-law lives in the house with the kids now. She takes care of them. You'll have to ask her. I guess."

"I thought that maybe if I got you to give me permission, then it might be easier. I'm assuming she's not interested in helping you?"

That made him laugh. "Oh, no. She hates my guts. I can't blame her. I would hate me too."

"That's what I'm hoping to be able to change," I said. "I hope to clear your name and give you your life back. I think you're innocent."

That made him laugh again. "You think I'm innocent?"

I nodded nervously. "Yes."

"You're crazy, do you know that?"

"I'll have to get used to being called that. I have a feeling I'll hear that a lot if I pursue this further."

He leaned back and gave me a suspicious look. "Are you even a real agent? You're pretty young."

I showed him my badge and photo ID. "But I am. A profiler."

"That looks brand new; how long have you had it?"

I blushed. "That's beside the point."

"Ah, I see. Young and eager to prove our worth, are we?"

"Maybe, but that shouldn't...."

"Tell me, why should I trust you?"

"Do you have a choice?" I asked, fighting to sound as confident as possible. "I don't see anyone else here trying to help you."

He shrugged. "I can say no."

"That's your choice, yes, of course. But then you'll have to rot in here for the rest of your life while sticking to your little lie that you killed your own wife."

Frank Woods paused. His smile went stiff, and he leaned back in his chair again. He stared at me for a few seconds, biting the inside of his cheek.

"I think our little chat is over."

"No, please," I said, placing a hand on the table. "I'm sorry if I offended you. I really need to do this. It's been driving me crazy. We went over your case during training, and it kept bothering me; it kept me awake at night."

Frank scoffed again. "Really?"

"Yes, really."

He narrowed his eyes. "You genuinely believe that I'm innocent?"

"Yes. That's what I've been trying to tell you all along."

"Even when I tell you that I'm not?"

"Yes."

He whistled. "Wow, either you're the smartest agent alive or the dumbest. I can't seem to figure out which one."

"Maybe let me be the judge of that," I said, grinning. I had been thinking the same thing repeatedly these past months when going over Frank's case in my mind, unable to let it go.

"So, what do you say? Will you give me access to your house and your things?" I asked hopefully.

He glared down at me. I couldn't blame him for being cynical. He had claimed his innocence for a long time, but no one believed him. In the end, he had finally told them he did it. I thought he had just caved because the pressure was too much, and he knew he couldn't win. That was one of my theories. Another was that he had admitted his guilt to protect someone else—someone dear to him. But I knew he would never tell me, so I didn't ask, at least not yet.

Then, he nodded. "Okay, little miss profiler. You have my permission. I'll have my lawyer write a letter to my sister-in-law and make sure she doesn't get in your way. Let's see what you can do."

That made me smile widely. "You won't regret it, Mr. Woods."

"I sure hope not," he said with a wink as the guards came back in and pulled him to his feet. He shuffled forward toward the door when he suddenly stopped and looked back at me.

"Let me ask you this, miss profiler... why my case? Of all the cases? Lots of people in here claim to be innocent. I don't. Why me? Why now?"

I sighed. I had asked myself that same question over and over again, trying to convince myself to leave it alone.

"Let's just say your profile didn't exactly fit this killer. As I said, we reviewed your case in class, and I didn't believe you did it at any point. I promised myself I'd take a closer look once I was hired. I don't think I can sleep until I do."

"You seem very sure, even though I say I killed her."

"I don't believe you. I know a liar when I see one."

That made him laugh, and as he was escorted out, he mumbled, "I like her."

# Chapter 4

He was watching the kids playing in the yard across the street. The little boy, who wasn't so little anymore as he neared the age of eight, was on the swings, while his older sister, by two years, was playing in the high grass with her small dolls.

Stefan Mark sighed deeply while seeing this. It wasn't often he got to see them anymore as they were playing more inside—probably watching TV or playing computer games like more and more children did these days. Or just tapping away on some mindless game on the phone. It saddened Stefan because he believed that children ought to spend time outside every day, as much as possible. Not that he had been a particularly outdoorsy kid himself, but still. He would like to see them more.

"Stop growing," he said and placed a hand on the window. "I can't keep up."

Stefan walked out on the porch with his coffee cup in his hand and sat down on the old porch swing. From here, he could hear the kids laughing, which was the most soothing sound in the world. How he wished he could go over there and hug them again like he used to. How he wished their little faces would light up and they'd run to him with open arms, yelling Uncle Stefan, and the little one would simply plop into his lap like the most natural thing in the world.

Like he belonged there.

But that was long ago now. Now, the kids only looked at him with big eyes like he was a stranger, and their aunt would pull them inside the house if he came near it. He was no longer welcome in their lives.

And that made him so sad.

Because he loved those little munchkins.

Stefan sipped his coffee while watching them play, enjoying the sound of their voices being carried across the cul-de-sac by the eastern wind. He couldn't hear exactly what they were saying, but they sounded happy, and that was enough for him. He stayed in this house for their sake, to be able to keep an eye on them and follow them as they grew. They were the only reason he hadn't left when the incident happened. This place brought him nothing but sorrow and deep sadness otherwise.

The girl, little Izzy, was playing quietly until her brother, Ben, jumped off the swing, ran to her, and took one of her dolls out of her hand. He took off laughing while Izzy screamed angrily. Then she got up and ran after him. Stefan watched them as she tried to catch him, and Ben squealed with joy, holding the doll up high in the air over his head so his sister couldn't reach it, even when jumping. In turn, Izzy pushed him hard, and he fell back, hitting his head on the asphalt driveway. Now, Ben was crying while Izzy triumphantly wriggled the doll out of his grip and was about to walk away when their aunt came running out to them. She helped Ben get up, then grabbed Izzy by the hand and pulled her forcefully toward the door while scolding her for pushing her brother. Stefan rose to his feet, feeling awful for poor Izzy, and as he did, their aunt turned her head and spotted him. Her eyes glared directly at him, and he felt it like icicles on his skin. Shivering, he turned around and went inside the house while Izzy cried on the other side of the cul-de-sac, being dragged toward the door.

# Chapter 5

It was past eight o'clock as I drove the car into the garage and closed it behind me. I grabbed my bag, then rushed into the kitchen. Chad didn't even look up from his computer screen as I entered.

"Am I too late?"

He finally lifted his gaze and met mine. "What?"

"The kids? I drove home as fast as I could to be able to tuck them in. Are they still up?"

"Oh, no, no," he said. "I put them to bed half an hour ago. They were being impossible and needed an early night. It's been a rough day. I'm exhausted."

I put my bag down. "Aw. I had hoped to be able to get to see them. They were still sleeping when I left this morning."

He shrugged, his eyes returning to the screen. "Well, our lives don't always revolve around your work schedule. The girls have to be in bed before eight, or they're impossible the next day; you know that."

"I know, but… I mean, it's just eight o'clock. I had hoped they'd stay up until…."

Chad gave me a look that made me stop.

"Right," I said, smiling reassuringly. "You had a rough day."

He shook his head. "You haven't the faintest idea. Trying to work with a two-year-old and a four-year-old running rampant in the house isn't exactly easy."

I frowned. "Didn't Christine and Olivia go to pre-school today?"

"Yes, but I wasn't done with work when I had to pick them up and thought I could finish it later, but there was constantly something. Not that you'd know what that's like."

"Oh, because I'm never home," I said and took off my jacket. "Way to make me feel welcome."

"Don't give me that. You're gone all day. I'm stuck here taking care of everything and my job."

"At least you get to work from home," I said, even though I wanted to stop the conversation now. I wasn't exactly in the mood, nor did I have the energy to have this talk again. I knew it would end the way it had so many times before.

Bad.

"Do you know what I'd give to be able to work from home? To be close to my kids?"

Chad scoffed and stared at his screen, clicking his mouse. I exhaled, feeling lonely. Not a kiss to greet me, not even a comforting word or a simple "how was your day." How had we come to this? We used to be so happy. Could it really all be because of my career? I knew I hadn't exactly been home much, but that was what we agreed on. We had talked it over when I started my training. That he would have to take care of a lot—well, most things—at home. It was the plan. He said he didn't mind. I was the breadwinner anyway. He didn't make much at his job selling home insurance. Especially not when the recession hit the year before. People couldn't afford to insure their houses, and many had to give up their homes completely and let the bank take over. The dropping housing market wasn't beneficial for a home insurance seller. And it was really hard on Chad, who struggled to make any money. Now, things were picking up slightly, but only slowly. I knew it bothered him, but he wouldn't admit it. Instead, he gave me a hard time as soon as I stepped through the door, and it was frankly getting a little old. I was sick of feeling guilty all the time for working and pursuing a career. I was inclined to ask him *what if it were the other way around?* What if it had been him pursuing a career and me staying home? He knew it would get difficult, and now all he could do was complain from the minute I entered until I left. He was always exhausted, always tired, and still the house looked like a mess, and I had to do the dishes before bedtime and clean up the toys in the living room. And I wasn't even going to see my girls. I got up at five-thirty in the morning to make it through the heavy D.C. traffic in time for my work, so I wouldn't see them in the morning either. The thought made me feel heavy.

Was it worth it?

I walked up the stairs, then peeked into the girls' bedroom. They each had their own room but insisted on sleeping together as they had always done back in the apartment we lived in before we bought the house.

"Why did we need this big house anyway, huh?" I mumbled. It was way too expensive for us, especially when Chad's salary was so unstable, but we had bought it right before the recession and thought money wouldn't be a problem. Now, the house had become like a chain around our legs, making things harder than they needed to be.

My girls were sleeping heavily, toys scattered all over the floor. Christine had her favorite big white bunny clutched tightly and slept with her mouth gaping because she had a cold. She was breathing heavily. I walked closer and smiled when seeing their beautiful faces. Nothing in the world could be better than this sight.

I turned to walk out when Olivia suddenly sat up. "Mom? Mommy?"

She rubbed her eyes and blinked.

"I'm sorry, sweetie. I didn't mean to wake you."

I hurried to her and hugged her tightly. "I missed you so much, Mommy," her little voice said into my ear. I felt like crying.

"I missed you too, baby."

"Why didn't you come home tonight?"

"I had work."

"Oh, yeah. Work is important."

"It really is, sweetie. But not more than you, don't you ever forget that."

That made her smile. "Daddy yelled at Christine tonight. He was really mad."

I sighed and hugged her small body. "We have to be nice to Daddy these days. He's doing the best he can."

She sniffled and nodded, rubbing her eyes. My little girl had gotten so big, and it was like she understood so much now. I held onto her while feeling scared that I was going to blink and she'd be grown up, slipping out of my hands. It was such a difficult choice to be the one that was always away. It filled me with deep guilt for pursuing my dream, yet I felt like I was just as much entitled to it as any man was.

Why wouldn't I be?

"I love you, Mommy."

Olivia closed her eyes, and I helped her lie down, then kissed her forehead and stroked her hair gently.

"I love you too. Tomorrow, I'll be home to tuck you in. I promise."

"Pinky promise?" she asked, half-asleep.

"Pinky promise," I said.

# Chapter 6

THEN:

It took several days before Ethan Weaver, as his name was, answered Mary Ellen's email. Mary Ellen checked her inbox every day and was surprised to see that he hadn't written her back. She had almost given up hope when, one evening, at eleven p.m., she finally received a reply from him. Almost trembling with anticipation and with bated breath, she clicked to open it. She read through it, her heart pounding harder and harder in her chest the further she got.

At first, he excused that it had taken him so long to answer, but he was out of the country and didn't check his inbox often. Then he told her about himself and how he had struggled after losing his sister, who died a few months ago, and that was why he had to go away for some time. Staying was simply too hard. He was very close with her since they grew up alone with their mother and brother after their father left, and he had to take care of his siblings when their mother was drunk, which was often. Mary Ellen read through the letter, feeling heavy-hearted, sobbing, and fighting her tears. She decided to reply right away. She told him about her own sister and how much she cared for her while they were children because their father was an alcoholic and would often beat them. She felt very protective of her still and couldn't imagine losing her. It would simply kill her. Then, as Mary Ellen finished the letter, she read through his again, feeling so close to this guy already. She couldn't help feeling like he needed her and that maybe she needed him too.

His reply came quickly this time, only two hours later.

*This is odd*, he wrote. *That we have so much in common—it's like the universe is telling us something here. Am I the only one feeling that? I have never felt this before. Is it strange? Am I too upfront for saying so already?*

Mary Ellen put a hand on her chest, feeling how her breathing had become strained the more she fought the feeling growing inside her. Then she wrote him back:

*Not at all. I feel it too, and I believe that when it's right, it's right, and there is no use in fighting it.*

He answered right away:

*I'm so glad to hear that. I don't want to come on too strong too soon, LOL. But the fact is, I really liked you from your first letter, and I felt like I could confide in you. These things don't come easy for me, and I have been disappointed so many times while online dating. It's weird, I know. But I feel like there's a real connection here. Please, let me know if you don't feel the same, and I'll back off.*

That made Mary Ellen smile widely. It was evening when she read it. She had poured herself a glass of wine and opened the computer after finally getting the kids to sleep after a long and strenuous day. The kids had been impossible, and she felt like she had been putting out fires all day. She was used to taking care of them by herself, but it still took its toll on her to have four of them between the ages of four and twelve. She really longed to have someone in her life besides them—someone who'd appreciate her, who'd tell her how beautiful she was, especially on days when she looked awful and felt even worse. She longed for someone to hold her hand at night, lie next to her, and whisper in her ear that everything would be all right; she was going to be okay. Together, they'd make it.

*Please, let Ethan be the one, please, God!*

She sipped from the glass, taking a deep breath to gather courage. Then she wrote:

*I do feel the same. I really do. I know it's fast, but why waste any time? Do you want to meet up one day?*

## Chapter 7

"This is a joke, right?"

The tall woman in front of me had her hair tied in a bun on top of her head. Her stern eyes stared down at me from inside the house. In her hand, she was holding the letter from Woods' lawyer that I had received from his office this same afternoon. I knew her name was Patricia Caplan and that she was Arlene Wood's sister, who took care of her children after her death.

"I mean, it has to be… right?" she continued.

I shook my head. "I assure you; this is serious."

A frown grew between her eyebrows. "You can't be… I mean, did you say you were from the FBI?"

I nodded again. "Yes, I'm working on reopening the case."

"Oh, no. No. No. No."

"I believe there has been a mistake."

She shook her head. "Oh, no, you don't. He killed my sister. He even admitted to it. He was convicted. It's over."

"I'm not saying he's not guilty. I'm just saying I would like to look through his and his wife's affairs, whatever is left."

"But… why?"

"Because I believe they missed something when they did the

25

investigation six years ago."

She gave me a look, mouth gaping. "You're telling me you believe he might be innocent? Is that what you're saying?"

She was getting angry with me now, and I knew I had to tread lightly here. I had to look at it from her point of view. Six years ago, she had lost her sister and fought to get her sister's husband convicted. It couldn't be pleasant to be asked to revisit that time or even suggest that he might be innocent—it had to hurt.

"I'm sorry," I said. "I realize this must be very painful, but…."

"Painful?" she shrieked. "You don't even know the half of it. I was the only one who knew he was guilty when everyone else thought Arlene had killed herself. She would never do that. She would never leave her children like that. Driving her car into a tree in the middle of the night? Oh, no. I knew he did this to her. I knew he was bad for her from the beginning. No one would listen to me."

"I understand," I said. "It can't have been easy."

Tears welled up in her eyes. Seeing it made me feel awful. I started to question what I was even doing here.

"Yeah, well…"

I tried to smile, but it came off unnatural, so I stopped. I looked at my watch and realized it was getting late.

"I'm sorry," I said. "But I need to take a look."

She scoffed. "I guess I don't have any other choice."

"I'm afraid not," I said.

Patricia sighed then stepped aside. She closed the door behind me as I walked inside. I could hear children's voices in the living room, and, as I passed, I spotted a boy and a girl sitting on the couch watching a movie. I smiled as Patricia led me to the stairs.

"It's in the attic. The police brought it back once the investigation was over, and I didn't know what to do with it all, so I kept it in the boxes they brought it back in and put it in the attic along with all the other stuff that was hers.

She pulled the string, and a ladder appeared. She pulled it down, then pointed.

"It's up there. Feel free to let yourself out when you're done. I have to make dinner for the children."

# Chapter 8

Stefan stirred the pot, the heat from it hitting his face. His cell buzzed on the counter next to him, and he looked at the display and the name with confusion.

"Patricia?"

"We need to talk."

"Listen, I know I was watching them. I'm sorry. I won't do it again."

"That's not why I'm calling," she said, almost whispering.

"It's not? Then what's going on? I haven't heard from you in years."

Patricia sighed on the other end. Stefan walked to the window and saw her out on her porch across the cul-de-sac. A black car he hadn't seen before was parked in her driveway.

"Patricia?" he asked nervously. "What's going on here?"

"There's someone here," she said. "From the FBI."

Stefan's eyes grew wide. He glanced at the car again, pulling the curtain completely aside. His heart started to beat faster.

"The FBI? What do they want?"

She was breathing heavily on the other end. "This woman... she appears to think that Frank might be... innocent."

"What?"

"You heard me. She thinks there might have been a mistake."

Stefan rubbed his forehead. "You can't be serious."

"That's what I said to her, but she is. She's young, though, and I have a feeling she's new on the job. Maybe no one will listen to her."

"Or maybe they will," Stefan said, fighting the panic rising in him. "What if she finds out?"

"Then we will deal with it," Patricia said.

Stefan went quiet. "You mean…?"

"I mean, we deal with it," Patricia hissed.

Stefan groaned. "We can't let them find out. You have to stop her."

"You need to calm down," Patricia said. "I don't think she'll find anything. If they didn't six years ago, then why would they do so now?"

Stefan eased up. Patricia was right. Why would some rookie suddenly find what the experienced investigators couldn't six years ago? This was just a scare—a bump in the road.

"There's nothing in those boxes, I assure you," she said. "I can't see what it would be?"

Stefan nodded. He closed his eyes briefly, then looked at the house across from him again. He had allowed himself to feel safe. It had taken years to get to this point where he had finally been able to put it all behind him. And now this? Now, it was all coming back? He wasn't going to let it happen.

"But you keep an eye on her, right?" he asked. "And keep me updated."

"Of course. I think she's coming down the stairs now. I have to hang up."

"All right," Stefan said. He wanted to say more, but the connection was lost. Patricia had hung up, and now he watched her go back inside the house. Stefan stared at the door as it closed behind her, then looked at the black car in the driveway, his heart beating fast in his chest. It felt like he couldn't breathe properly, and he clasped his chest and sat down in the recliner next to the window, focusing on breathing. He closed his eyes and leaned back, trying to think of something else. But all he could hear was his own voice screaming inside him: *I can't go through this again. I simply can't! Will this ever end?*

# Chapter 9

Chad was in the kitchen when I came home. I walked in through the door to the garage, and when his eyes landed on me, I knew I had messed up. He had his arms crossed in front of his chest, and everything about his posture told me he was angry with me.

It took a few seconds before I remembered.

"Oh, shoot. Olivia."

"So, you do remember that you have children?"

I put down my bag. "That's not fair. I hurried home as fast as I could."

"Maybe you shouldn't make promises then. Maybe you shouldn't tell your daughter that you'll come home and tuck her in when you can't. When you come home an hour and a half later than her bedtime."

I exhaled, tired. "I'm so sorry. Was she very upset?"

"She refused to go to bed for the first half-hour, then when I finally persuaded her to go, she kept crying for you. She was inconsolable. She kept saying that you'd pinky promised to be here, that you'd come soon."

"Because a pinky promise is unbreakable," I mumbled, feeling heavy in my heart. Nothing was worse than the guilt from not being there for your children.

"I'll go talk to her and say I'm sorry," I said.

"You're not going up there now. I just got her to fall asleep," he said. "You're not ruining all the work I did tonight."

I slumped my shoulders, feeling awful. I knew he was right, even though it was painful. I wanted so badly to tell her just how sorry I was.

"Okay," I said. "I'll talk to her in the morning."

"You usually leave before they get up," he said.

"That's right. Well, maybe I'll go in a little later tomorrow morning and make breakfast for all of us. How does that sound?"

Chad tilted his head. "That sounds like something you can't do. What about work?"

"My supervisor dumped a pile of cases on my desk earlier today that need profiling, but she'll just have to wait a little."

I sat down and grabbed a piece of the cold pizza on the counter, even though I knew I shouldn't. I hadn't had much time to work out these past few months, and it was beginning to show. Especially after my second pregnancy, I needed to be more careful as I tended to bulge out around my stomach. Before I had children, I was a runner, and I would run every morning, but now there simply was no time.

"I thought you were working on that old case you talked about?" he asked. "The one that has bothered you for years?"

I took another bite and chewed. "I am, but I'm doing that when I have a break between other cases. I don't have enough yet to bring it up for reopening, so I need to find that first."

"It's extra work? On top of what's expected of you?"

I nodded and finished the piece, then grabbed another as my guilt nagged in the pit of my stomach.

"Let me get this straight. When you tell me you came home late because of work, it's something you chose to do? Not something they're forcing you to do?"

I stopped chewing. "Well, when you put it that way, you make it sound awful."

"It sort of is, Eva Rae. You're choosing this work and neglecting your family because of it. It is awful."

I swallowed. "An innocent man might be spending his life in prison. That's what is awful," I said and got up. "But I don't expect you to understand that."

# Chapter 10

**T** HEN:
    She had never been so nervous. Mary Ellen had agreed to meet Mr. Perfect in a restaurant downtown. She had picked the place to make sure she felt safe. Meeting up with a guy from a dating site was, after all, still filled with some uncertainty. There were so many stories about women being raped or kidnapped that she knew she had to be cautious. She had met with several men she had found on this site, and so far, she had been disappointed every time.

But Ethan was different. She was so sure of it. It just felt different. The way they talked when writing to one another was special. She had set the expectations high; she knew it perfectly well, and that was dangerous. She could only pray he'd live up to them.

They had moved away from the website pretty fast and started to talk on text. Then she had told him to send more pictures of himself, to feel safer, and he had sent some that had seemed almost professionally made. In one of them, he was standing by his kayak, bare-chested and looking like a model in a magazine. She had then wondered if it was really him in those pictures—so handsome with blond hair and blue eyes; it seemed almost impossible.

Then she had asked if they could call. She wanted to talk to him before they met—to hear his voice and feel him out. He had called right away. He had even been shy and so cute it was almost too much. How could one man be this perfect?

They had talked on the phone every day since, and now it was time to meet up in real life for an actual date. Mary Ellen was so nervous as she entered the restaurant; it almost hurt in her stomach.

But as soon as she entered through the glass door, she saw his eyes as he looked up from the bar where he was sitting and waiting. When their eyes met, he smiled gently, and she did as well. In that instant, it felt like they had known each other forever—like they already knew everything there was to know. It was almost like they shared a life of secrets.

"I got us a table by the window," he said and reached out his hand.

Mary Ellen blushed as he came closer, realizing all eyes in the restaurant were on him. All the women wanted to be with him, and all the guys wanted to be him.

Ethan held out the chair for her, and she sat down, still with everyone's eyes on her and her man. This, she wasn't used to. Her ex-husband had been a wealthy lawyer from a stinking rich family, but he was far from handsome. Michael hadn't been first in line when God gave out looks, that was for sure. But he had been sweet and kind, at least to begin with, until he showed his true colors after she had given birth to four of his children and left her for another man. She should have seen the warning signs earlier on; she knew that. And if she didn't, then her mother sure told her so.

"You must have known; I mean, when you guys... in bed?"

"Mom, stop."

Mary Ellen shook her head, trying to get the thought out of her mind. She hated to think of Michael and their marriage. Michael had left her with four children and never looked back. He didn't even show up for birthdays, not even a card. Not to mention the alimony he hadn't paid in years. It was all such a mess, and Mary Ellen didn't want to deal with it anymore. She hoped that meeting a new guy and maybe eventually getting married again would wipe out her entire past. She hoped that Ethan was just that guy. As he smiled at her across the table and looked deeply into her eyes, she couldn't help feeling like he could be it. He had told her he had money, and that was a huge plus. By the look of the expensive suit he was wearing, he was telling the truth.

"I'm so glad we finally did this," he said. He had a slight accent that he had told her was from growing up with Swedish parents that immigrated to the U.S. when he was seven years old. It sounded cute and only made him more attractive.

"Me too," she said with a deep sigh. She was relieved that so far, there were no red flags. She still kept her guard up, though. After all, it had taken years for Michael to show her who he really was, and according to her mother, it was just because she hadn't paid enough attention. She wasn't going to make that same mistake again.

Ethan reached out his hand toward hers, then paused and looked up at her. "Is it okay if I hold your hand? I've longed to know what that feels like."

Mary Ellen blushed again.

"Y-yes. Of course."

He smiled and looked down. Then, he grabbed her hand in his. Warmth spread up through her, and she shivered slightly at the touch.

It was true what they said. It felt like electricity.

"Are you okay?" he asked, studying her face.

"Yes, it's just... this is really nice. Is it okay to say that?"

"Yes," he said with a chuckle. "It's more than okay. I feel like I've known you forever, yet I'm still so nervous."

"I know," she said. "Me too. I've been so scared all day."

"Because everything up until now has been so perfect."

Her eyes lit up.

"Exactly. I was so sure I was going to be disappointed. If you knew how many times I have...."

"Been on dates that turned out horribly? Yeah, me too."

"Oh, no, I think I'll have you beat on this one," she said and sipped her wine that the waiter just poured them. "No one has better stories than me."

He laughed, then leaned forward. "Try me. I bet I have worse stories."

"I don't believe you."

The next few hours, while working their way through dinner, they each told their stories, one more terrifying than the other, and they both couldn't help laughing. Mary Ellen noticed that Ethan barely drank anything, only sipped his wine, and as the night progressed, she was getting tipsy while he was still sober.

"Let me take you home," he asked as they walked outside the restaurant. "Please? I don't want this night to end."

"All right," she smiled after thinking it over for a few seconds. Then she let him escort her to his Lexus in the parking lot.

# Chapter 11

"**Y**ou again?"

I nodded, then held up the letter from Frank Woods' lawyer. It was late afternoon, and I was done with my other cases when I left to take another look at this one, even though it made me feel guilty about Chad. He clearly thought I should leave this alone. But he just didn't understand that simply wasn't a possibility for me. Not if I wanted a good night's sleep again. And I had spent the morning with them, making pancakes and bacon after telling Olivia how sorry I was for not keeping my promise.

"I thought you were done?" Patricia asked. "It's really a bad time."

"I'm far from done," I said. "There are a lot of boxes."

Patricia sighed. "You're not gonna find anything. I hope you realize that. And you know why?"

"Because you believe he's guilty?"

"Bingo. He killed my sister and tried to make it look like suicide."

"Well, I still have my reasons to believe he didn't do it," I said. "And I intend to prove it."

37

Patricia sighed, then showed me inside. She walked with me up the ladder to the boxes, then crossed her arms in front of her chest.

"Mind if I ask why?"

I opened a box with Arlene's name on the side and took out a pile of books. I looked at the titles, then put them down and reached inside again.

"Why what?"

"Why do you think he's innocent?" she said. "The rest of the world seems to disagree with you. Even him."

I looked up. "He's lying. Maybe to protect someone."

"And why are you so certain of this?"

I paused, then continued, pulling out more books and some notebooks that I flipped through.

"I just am."

Patricia scoffed. "You got nothing. Did he pay you or something? Did he offer you a bunch of money to prove his innocence? Because I got news for you, he's got no money, as in none at all."

I looked up briefly, then shook my head. "Nope. He didn't offer me anything. I'm doing this because I think he is innocent. And that means somewhere out there is a murderer who never got caught. That's all I can focus on right now."

Patricia stared at me, biting the side of her cheek. "You're crazy."

"Maybe you're right," I said with a light shrug. "But I guess that's my problem, not yours, right?"

"Do you even know what you're looking for? Or are you just trying all the angles?"

I paused and looked down into the box. She had me there. I wasn't sure what I was expecting to find at all, but I had to start somewhere, right?

"I can't disclose that, I'm afraid," I said, hoping to shut her up.

Patricia scoffed again.

"I thought as much."

"Again, my problem, not yours."

"Well, it is my problem since you come here and disturb the kids and me constantly. What do you want me to tell them? That you want to reopen the case and have the man who killed their mother acquitted?"

"Listen, I know it can't be easy, but still. Wouldn't you want the real murderer found? What if this person has done this to others or is about to? Do you want this person to get away with it? Don't you want justice for Arlene?"

"I do, and I did," Patricia hissed. "We went through so much to get Frank convicted. Months and months of investigation and then the trial. These kids have been through enough, and so have I."

I looked at her, then felt my heart drop. She was right. It was a lot for me to ask them to go through it all again, and I didn't like doing that to the children.

"Do you have children?" she asked me.

"Yes."

"So, you're a mother," Patricia said. "How can you justify this? Putting the kids through hell again? And for what? To let a murderer out? I know he killed her. I knew it from the moment she met him—that he was going to hurt her. She wouldn't listen to me. She never would listen to her sister. I'm not just going to let you destroy it all with your little hunches or whatever it is you've got going."

Patricia breathed heavily as one of the children called her name from downstairs, and she left. I felt a sigh of relief go through me as I watched her leave. I couldn't really work with her constantly hovering above me. I needed space and quiet if I were to find what no one else had been able to so far.

I needed a clue to find out who really killed Arlene Woods on that fatal night when her car slammed into a tree on Wisconsin Avenue at four in the morning, and I was asking the question no one else seemed to have in this case.

Why was she out driving in the middle of the night? She had left her two children at home sleeping. Where was she going?

I was hoping to find out while going through her belongings, but it seemed all to be in vain so far. Until I picked up one of the books, and it slipped out of my hands. It fell and unfolded on the first page. I picked it up, then looked at it and realized it had an inscription.

Someone had given her this book, then written a greeting inside it. That wasn't unusual and shouldn't have gotten my attention.

But the wording did. What it said was very disturbing.

I stared at it, then looked around to see if I was still alone. I was, so I grabbed the book and put it inside my bag, heart throbbing in my chest. I went through a couple of other books, then put them in my bag as well. I closed the box, grabbed the bag, and went down the ladder. I rushed down the stairs toward the front door, then Patricia came up behind me.

"Leaving so soon?"

I nodded, my hand lingering on the bag across my shoulder.

"Yes. I need to get home to the kids."

She scoffed. "I told you that you wouldn't find anything."

I smiled, then nodded secretively.

"Thanks for your help anyway."

# Part II

## TWO WEEKS LATER

# Chapter 12

Mindy Lynn stared at the flat-screen TV on the wall in front of her at Walmart. A woman pushed her cart around her with an annoyed scoff. She was blocking the aisle, as she had stopped pushing her cart when seeing the headlines in front of her. She couldn't hear what the news anchor said, but the text was enough for her to stop, her hands shaking while trying to hold onto the handle of the cart.

FBI TO CONSIDER REOPENING CASE AGAINST FRANK WOODS.

The words were in the yellow box below the anchor's pretty face and moving lips, and it was all Mindy needed to know exactly what was happening.

A woman pushed her cart close to Mindy's, then said, "Excuse me," and made her way through.

"I'm sorry," Mindy said and looked after the woman who was already far down the aisle. Mindy grabbed her cell, then rushed out of the store, leaving behind the cart with all her groceries inside it. She pressed a number, then ran to her car and got in.

"Mindy, what the heck?"

"Did you see? The news?" she said, panting agitatedly. "Tuck? Did you see it?"

"What... what on earth are you talking about? I haven't heard from you in years, and you just call out of the blue and make no sense?"

"I just saw it myself. They say they're considering reopening the case against Frank Woods."

Tuck went quiet. Mindy could hear a female voice in the background and then Tuck hushing her. She knew he had another woman now. She didn't mind. After that night, she hadn't been able to be anywhere near him, and they had separated not long after. She had begged him to call the cops back then when they saw the car crash, but he hadn't wanted to.

"So, what?" he said now. "Why do you care? It's been six years."

"But... shouldn't we tell them the truth?"

"Listen," he said. "We were drunk as skunks that night. That's why we didn't call the police. That hasn't changed. How will you explain to them now that we didn't say anything back then without telling them we were drunk driving?"

Mindy exhaled. "I've just... it's torturing me, Tuck. I can't stand knowing what we do and not telling them. I can't stand to be lying. It's not right."

"Mindy, it's too late now. It's been six years, for crying out loud. You need to move on. Besides, we made a promise, remember?"

Mindy felt her heart drop. She bit her lip, wondering if she could keep it, keep this big secret when knowing it might change everything if she told the truth.

"Mindy," Tuck said with a stern voice. "You're keeping your mouth shut, do you hear me?"

"But... Tuck..."

"I'm telling you. Don't start ripping up that old story. It's closed. The guy was put away."

"But they don't know the truth," she said. "And we can give them that. They must be onto it since they're considering reopening the case."

Tuck sighed, annoyed. She knew exactly what he looked like

when he did that. You didn't date someone for seven years without knowing exactly what they looked like when annoyed. She realized she didn't miss him at all, even though she had been alone since they separated.

"Just don't. Okay?" he said harshly. "I have to go now. But you keep your mouth shut. You hear me?"

"I don't know if I can," she said and hung up before he could protest. He tried to call her back a second later, but she left it ringing in her purse. She threw it on the seat next to her, turned the key, and roared the car back to life, not even noticing the car following her all the way back to her apartment.

# Chapter 13

"Care to explain this?"

I looked up from the computer screen in my cubicle. Above me stood FBI Director Isabella Horne. She was an extremely beautiful woman who made people shiver by her presence. Not so much because of her beauty but because she was known to kill a career with a snap of her finger. I had only seen her at the Behavioral Analysis Unit, the BAU, once before, and that was to tell a colleague to pack his stuff and leave. I didn't know why he was fired and didn't ask since I had only been at Quantico briefly at that point. Well, I was still the freshest face there, and therefore ranked lowest in the hierarchy.

Now, she was looking directly at me, her brown eyes ablaze.

In her hand, she was holding an iPad that she turned so I could see the headlines in the post. Horne lifted both her eyebrows.

"This is the moment when you start talking."

My heart was beating fast in my chest.

"I... I..."

"You're new here, so let me explain to you how things work. No one, and I mean no one, reopens a case without me knowing it. No one. And no one tells the press about it before they come to me either."

"But I didn't...."

"Now, I spoke to your supervisor, Terry, and he tells me he didn't authorize this reopening. He told me he said you ought to leave this alone and stay with the profiling cases he has given you."

I could barely breathe. This woman was terrifying.

"You do realize you're a profiler, right?" she continued, not giving me the time to defend myself. "Do we need to go over your job description again? You're an analyzer. You're supposed to read reports and analyze them. You tell investigators what they're looking for based on your analyses. You don't do field work."

"Of course not. I've been doing it on my own time," I said. "And I never said anything to the press. I don't know where they got the story. But it does say the FBI is *considering* reopening the case, and no one can say we aren't. At least I am. And I think you will be soon, too."

Horne's expression changed to one of confusion. "On your own time? What's that supposed to mean?"

"It means I can't sleep because of this case, and I won't rest until I'm certain there hasn't been a mistake."

Horne paused while scrutinizing me. "You're seriously questioning what experienced investigators have concluded and what the court has convicted?"

I nodded determinedly. "Yes. I think there was a mistake made six years ago. I believe they missed something important."

Horne laughed, then stopped. "You're serious? How long have you been here in this unit?"

"Four weeks. Since I was done with my training, but I've worked on it for years in my mind. I know I'm right about this."

A frown grew between her eyebrows. "You don't do normal, do you?"

I shook my head. "No, ma'am."

She stared down at me but kept silent for a few seconds.

"All right, little miss '*I'm certain there has been a mistake,*' so, what have you got? Sell it to me before I kick you out of here for going behind my back."

# Chapter 14

T HEN:
 Mary Ellen was floating on a pink cloud of happiness. She had never felt this way before about a guy. It seemed impossible to be this much in love. Luckily, he was feeling the same. Every morning, he called her to say good morning, and then again at lunchtime to hear how she was doing, see if she needed anything, and then he called again before bedtime to say goodnight. Sometimes, they'd hang on and talk way into the night, making Mary Ellen exhausted the next day, but it didn't matter. Nothing else mattered at this point but him. She counted the hours until they saw one another again, and he said he did too when sending her flowers or chocolates or small surprises, like a scented candle or a bracelet. Every day, there was something from him, and she almost came to expect him to shower her with gifts, even though she tried really hard to remind herself not to take it for granted.

This was special and had to be enjoyed. After all, not many women got to experience such a big love like this.

*I'm the luckiest woman on the planet,* she thought as she once again closed the door on the flower guy who had just handed her another bouquet of red roses. She smelled them and smiled widely, then read the card where Ethan wrote how much he was looking forward to seeing her that same night, and then the name of the restaurant where he had reserved a table.

"Are you falling for him?" her best friend Arianna had asked the day before when calling. "Like really falling in love?"

"I think so. At first, I was a little reluctant because I felt like he talked about money a lot," she had said. "Like he would tell me about the money he made on different investments like he expected me to be impressed with it, and he'd tell me he had a lot of money in an account in Europe, stuff like that, but it was actually quite the turn off for me. I didn't like that part about him in the beginning."

"What changed?"

"He stopped talking about it," Mary Ellen said. "And then we went on a date at the carnival downtown, and as we sat down and ate cotton candy, he really opened up to me. He began talking about his mom and how he misses her since she lives in Poland, and he hasn't seen her in a long time."

"Poland? Wait a minute; wasn't he from Sweden?"

"His dad is, but his mom is Polish, apparently. And she moved back some years ago after Ethan and his siblings left home. She's with some new guy now, he says. And he can't stand him, so that's why he doesn't go so often. But he has a lot of business over there, and she runs it for him, along with his half-brother."

"Sounds complicated. But at least he has money, and as long as you're happy…."

"I am. I really am. And I'm afraid I'm in way deeper than I thought at first. Just thinking about him makes my stomach flutter."

Mary Ellen thought about her conversation with her friend as she got ready for their next date, still feeling the butterflies. She hadn't slept with Ethan yet, only kissed him, and she wondered if she might do it tonight. She felt very certain of him and their love for one another, and to be honest, she really wanted to be with him. She had thought about it so much lately and wasn't sure she could wait any longer.

A light knock on her door made her jump to her feet in anticipation. It was him. This was the night to do it.

She was ready.

# Chapter 15

"Arlene Woods died on September 27th, 2003. Initially, it was believed she died when her car crashed into a tree on Wisconsin Avenue at four in the morning and caught on fire. But a later autopsy told the investigators that she was already dead at the time of impact. In fact, they determined the time of death to be a half hour earlier, and the cause of death was a stab wound to her heart. They concluded she was stabbed inside the car since she was an hour away from her home, and when she left the house, she was seen by a neighbor passing by, which means she was still alive."

I paused and looked at Horne sitting next to me. She and I had come into a conference room so that I could present the case to her properly. She was giving me one chance to sell this to her. She was listening closely with reserved curiosity while I bit my tongue so she wouldn't see how nervous I was. This was it for me. If I couldn't convince her this was worth reopening, then I was done in the unit. I would either be asked to leave, or they would park me somewhere in a corner and never give me an interesting assignment again.

This was a *make it or break it* kind of moment, and I had a feeling I wasn't doing very well so far. By the look on Horne's face, she was far from impressed.

"All this we already know," she said, looking at her watch. "You're still failing to catch my interest in this, and you only have a few more minutes before I have to be somewhere else."

I took a deep breath. "I'll get to the point."

She snapped her fingers. "Please do and a little faster."

"Okay, to put it briefly, Frank Woods doesn't fit the profile," I said. "That's what got me interested."

"Okay, and why not?"

"He was Arlene's husband for six years. Murderers who kill intimate partners and family members have a significantly different psychological and forensic profile from murderers who kill people they don't know."

"Go on."

"Take the motive," I said.

"They were heading for a divorce," she said. "He got angry when he found out she had an affair. They were in an argument that night. He got drunk. He said all this when he confessed."

"Yet this was premeditated murder. The knife was concluded possibly to be a hunting knife. Frank never went hunting; he wasn't outdoorsy."

"Could have been something else."

"Yes, but it was planned. The forensic report also concluded that she died from just one stab of the knife. Whoever stabbed her knew what he was doing and that she would die from just that one stab. And it wasn't done in anger because then…."

"There would have been multiple stab wounds."

"We see jealousy attacks where they have seventeen even up to thirty stab wounds because they lose themselves in the moment, in the anger. This wasn't a result of domestic violence. There were no broken bones or signs of violence otherwise on the body. Frank Woods was never in the army, nor did he have any training in killing. He's a dad and family man. He worked as an insurance agent. He never laid a hand on Arlene or the kids before. There's no history of violence."

"He is an alcoholic, though," Horne said. "He said he was drinking heavily on the night he murdered her."

"True, but look at this," I said and flipped through the pages in some of the folders. "All this isn't the profile of a domestic homicide. I mean, evidence found in the car concluded that her body had been covered in gasoline before being set on fire. This person wanted to make sure she was burnt, so it would look like she died in the crash. That is really calculated. This guy knew what he was doing."

"So, what are you saying?"

"It can't be his first kill. I think this guy has done it before. And I fear he's gonna do it again."

Horne went quiet, staring at the papers in front of us. She was tapping her fingers on the wooden conference table.

"Okay, I see your point. But it is still far from enough to reopen a case, especially one that was so high-profile back then and that the media will throw themselves at if it turns out a mistake was made."

"There's more," I said. I reached into my bag and pulled out four books. I opened them to the pages with their inscriptions, then showed them to Horne one after the other.

"I found these among Arlene's stuff in her attic."

Horne read the handwritten inscriptions, then looked up at me, mouth gaping. "Someone was trying to warn her?"

I nodded. "Someone sent these to her. Someone else knew her life was in danger. This person is telling her to be cautious. And it isn't about her husband. You wouldn't refer to him as 'the man you are seeing.'"

Horne nodded slowly and pensively. "I'll be...."

"And that leads me back to the question I've been asking myself since I heard about this case the first time."

"And that is?"

I cleared my throat. "Where was Arlene going in the middle of the night? Who was she going to meet? What mom leaves her house and her sleeping children at three in the morning?"

"Okay," Horne said. "Say I buy into this. Then tell me this. Why was Frank seen walking back to the house at around six in the morning by not one but two neighbors? And then the really big question: why has he confessed to killing her?"

I bit my cheek. "I don't have an answer for that yet, but that's what I want to find out. Someone is lying in this case, and I need to figure out who."

Horne leaned back in her chair, folding her hands behind her head while her cell phone vibrated on the table. She wasn't picking it up. That was a good sign. I had caught her attention.

She finally reached down her hand and took it, then looked at me before she pressed the button.

"Don't make me regret this, Eva Rae, do you hear me? And keep the press out of it, for crying out loud."

She got up and left, phone pressed against her ear, while I sat back, my hands still shaking heavily, a smile spreading across my lips, butterflies still fluttering in my stomach.

I got my chance. I couldn't believe it. Now, I just had to make sure I didn't waste it.

# Chapter 16

Mindy rushed up the stairs and locked herself inside her small townhouse. She put her purse down, then hurried to the kitchen. She glanced over her shoulder for a second like she expected someone to be there, even though she lived alone. Heart beating hard in her chest, she opened the cabinet and reached in behind the cups, searching with her fingers. Inside a jar in the back, she touched something and picked it up. She pulled it out and looked at it in her hand. It was so small, yet it held so much power.

Heart throbbing, she put it inside her jacket, then closed the cabinet when she heard a noise behind her. With a light gasp, she turned around, but no one was there. She breathed, relieved again.

*It was just your imagination. You need to calm down.*

Mindy felt the device in her pocket while sweat sprang to her forehead. Should she bury it in the backyard? Or should she take it to the police like she was supposed to six years ago, but Tuck talked her out of it?

*You keep your mouth shut. You hear me?*

Those were his words to her back then and again earlier today. Tuck was determined to keep quiet about what they knew. Mindy wasn't sure she could do that. She really wanted to get this off her chest. It was torture to have this knowledge and keep it to herself.

"I can't do it," she mumbled under her breath. "I can't do it anymore. I'm really sorry, Tuck."

Mindy sighed heavily. Her going to the police would mean betraying her promise to Tuck, and it wasn't going to be fun; that was for sure. She would probably get in trouble herself for not coming forward earlier. And she didn't know what kind of trouble Tuck might end up in, being drunk and all while driving. It might get ugly. But then again, how would they know? It wasn't like they could nail him for drunk driving six years later when they didn't have any proof. Didn't they need to have a blood test or something like that? Why didn't he just lie and say he was in shock, and that's why they drove off? Was he afraid they might think he was involved somehow? She never understood his argument, especially not now six years later. No one would find out what they had done. And no matter what, nothing could be worse than living with this nagging feeling in the pit of her stomach. It was driving her nuts, and it had to stop.

"I'm doing it."

She turned to grab her purse and keys when footsteps approached her, and someone suddenly stood in front of her.

"I wouldn't do that if I were you."

Mindy couldn't breathe, staring into the eyes of the person in front of her. Those eyes were piercing straight through her. The person acted fast and stepped forward, then slammed a fist into her cheek, causing her to stumble back, hitting her back against the kitchen counter. A loud crack sounded, and pain shot through her. Mindy screamed and slid to the kitchen floor as the person stepped closer, then knelt in front of her.

# Chapter 17

I t smelled heavenly when I stepped in through the front door. I knew why immediately, and it made me smile. I had seen my mother-in-law's old purple 1987 Chevy Silverado pick-up truck parked in our driveway and knew she was here. Miranda was Chad's mother, but she had become just as much mine over the years, maybe even more, to be honest. She lived on a farm sixty miles outside of D.C. in a small, charming town—if you liked the rural areas—called Boonsboro. She was an old hippie with a long silver mane, who believed in my right to a career and supported me, while my own mother, who lived in Cocoa Beach, Florida with my dad, where I was born and raised, thought I was destroying my family by following my selfish needs. Needless to say, those two never did well when in a room together, which luckily rarely happened. I wasn't very close with my mom and couldn't get far enough away from her when I was ready to leave home. She never knew how to handle me, especially not after my sister Sydney was kidnapped from a supermarket when I was five and she was seven, and we never saw her again. Sydney had been her favorite child, and even though she never admitted it, she blamed me for what happened that day. I knew she did, and I had felt it through my entire childhood.

"Grandma is here," Olivia squealed as I walked into the kitchen. I spotted Miranda by the stove, stirring the pot, her silver mane in a ponytail. I loved her cooking, and even though it was hard to admit, I was actually happier to see her than Chad standing in my kitchen.

"I see that."

Olivia ran to me, and I picked her in my arms, then kissed her cheeks until she giggled. Christine said something no one understood, then hurried to me, and I picked her up in my arms.

"You're home earlier than expected," Miranda said, turning to face me. "Chad told me you'd be late."

I kissed her cheek and took a deep breath.

"I was able to get out earlier, and now I'm sure glad I did. Oh, it smells heavenly."

"I brought herbs from the yard and homegrown fresh tomatoes. Lamb chops are from the farm too."

"Wonderful. I'm starving." A plate of Miranda's famous home-baked cookies was on the dining table, and I grabbed one to crunch the worst of my hunger. "So, where is Chad?"

Miranda looked at me, narrowing her eyes. "He didn't tell you I was coming tonight?"

I bit into the cookie. Christine tried to grab it from my hand, and I let her have a bite. "I might have forgotten."

Miranda looked troubled. "He had some meeting that was going to run into the evening. He told me a week ago."

I shrugged and smiled at Christine in my arms while chewing the cookie. "He probably told me at the same time. I have a lot on my mind these days. It probably just slipped; you know how it is."

"Are you sure you two are okay?" Miranda asked while chopping carrots. "Not that it is any of my business."

I grabbed another cookie and bit into it while setting Christine down on the floor to run to her toys.

"Yeah, we're fine. Just busy with everything, the kids and jobs and all that."

My eyes avoided Miranda's, and she noticed. I smiled nervously, and she continued chopping.

"If you say so."

# Chapter 18

**T**HEN:
The sex was everything Mary Ellen had hoped it would be. Ethan was every bit as well built as he had been in the pictures he posted. Not that she doubted him, but it just seemed almost too good to be true.

Mary Ellen put her head on the pillow and sighed deeply, smiling from ear to ear. Her kids were with her mother tonight, so she didn't have to worry about them meeting him yet. But now that she knew they were compatible sexually, she felt more confident in a possible future together.

Ethan got up and went to the bathroom, his skin still glistening with sweat. Mary Ellen watched him go by and took another last glance at his behind as he disappeared into the bathroom. Then she grabbed a pillow and placed it on her head while releasing a satisfied moan.

How could any one man be this perfect?

*Just enjoy it, will you?*

Her best friend had said the same thing. If it felt good—if he really was all he had seemed to be, why not just have some fun?

Why worry? Why be looking for things that can go wrong? Why keep searching for faults with him?

Ethan came back in and crawled into bed with her again, kissing her neck and shoulder. Mary Ellen closed her eyes and breathed heavily. His lips were so soft, and those deep blue eyes staring at her felt like he could see straight into her soul—her deepest hidden secrets. And yet it didn't feel invasive when he looked at her, when he scrutinized her, observed her. It almost felt like she had known those eyes for her entire life. They felt familiar.

Safe.

"Why do you keep looking at me?" she asked with a soft smile.

He groaned. "Mmm. I just want to take you in, all of you. And keep a mental picture for my trip."

Mary Ellen's smile froze. "Trip? What trip?"

He laughed and put his finger on her nose. "My trip to Poland, silly."

She sat up.

"I don't think I've heard about that before?"

He sat on the edge of the bed, grabbed his boxers, and put them on. He laughed, then arched an eyebrow at her.

"Yes, you have. I told you last week."

Mary Ellen stared at him while he picked up his jeans from the chair, where he had folded them and placed them before they had sex.

"I think I would have remembered that."

"I would like to think that you did," he said. "I'd like to imagine that I am that important to you."

Mary Ellen stared at him, feeling confused. Had he told her? Maybe he did say something on their last date. She had been drinking wine, and perhaps it just slipped her mind? Oh, she felt so embarrassed.

Mary Ellen shook her head. "I guess I must have forgotten. How long will you be gone?"

"Just a month this time," he said as he leaned over and kissed her forehead.

"A-a month?"

He shook his head. "It's just business. Believe me; I'd rather stay here with you."

"But...I thought you were retired?"

He shrugged, then smiled softly, tilting his head.

"I am. But I still have investments I need to keep an eye on. Don't bother your pretty head with all this. Time will fly by faster than you think, and before you know it, I'll be back here again and in your arms."

"But..."

"I have to go," he said as he kissed her cheek, then whispered, "Love you."

She stared at him as he grabbed his shirt, put it on, and left, waving at her. As the door closed, she still sat there, staring at the spot where he had disappeared, wondering: *Did he just say he loved me?*

# Chapter 19

"You could have reminded me this morning when I kissed you goodbye."

I was in the bathroom, brushing my teeth. Chad had come home, and Miranda left after I put the kids to sleep. I spat in the sink.

"I was still asleep," he said. "And to be honest, I thought you remembered I was going to a meeting out of town and therefore couldn't make it home in time to pick up the kids at daycare. And I knew you wouldn't be able to. That's why I called Mom."

"I might have been able to," I said. "I don't think you even asked me."

"Well, I'm sorry, but normally you can't, so I just assumed…"

"Don't assume, please," I said and rinsed my toothbrush in the water from the tap. "I know I don't often come home in time, but at least ask because some days I might be able to."

Chad sighed. "Yeah, whatever."

I rinsed my mouth and spat. "What's that supposed to mean?"

"Nothing."

"It didn't sound like nothing."

"Does it matter?" he asked, throwing out his arms. "I've had a long day. I just want to go to sleep. The kids will be demanding early in the morning, and you'll have left. Again."

I stared at him in the mirror. I felt my heart drop. I had talked to Miranda about my guilt tonight, and she had said that I couldn't have it all. If I chose the career, then good for me, but I couldn't expect my marriage to be perfect or to be there for my children in every matter. It was not humanly possible.

"But that's okay," she had added. "The kids don't lack anything. They have everything they need, and they get to grow up seeing their mother making a difference in the world. That's worth a lot too. Don't be so hard on yourself. There's nothing wrong with the dad pulling the weight. He is just as much a parent as you."

"I just hate it when I go places and people ask me, 'So, is your husband helping with the kids?' Like the responsibility is mine alone, and he is just helping out."

That made Miranda laugh.

"Oh, yes. It's not like people would ask him that."

I put my toothbrush back in place, then turned to face Chad. "I know there's been a lot on your shoulders lately."

"Yeah, well, I wouldn't mind if you'd let me have my way."

"What do you mean?"

He looked at me secretively. "You know what I really want?"

"I'm not sure I do."

He came closer and grabbed me around the waist. He was smiling, and that wasn't like him these days, so I became suspicious.

"I know that look. I'm not gonna like this, am I?"

He shrugged. "You might enjoy it."

I paused. "Not that again. Chad, I told you I don't want to."

I pushed him away and walked past him. "I told you I don't want any more children."

"Why not? We've never been happier than when we had the other two."

I crawled under the covers with a deep sigh. "I thought you understood, Chad. I can't. I've just gotten the career I wanted so badly. I can't take time off now. Plus, I don't want any more children. Don't you think we have enough as it is? I mean, you're always complaining about how hard it is."

He crawled into bed and came up close to me, kissing my neck.

"Yeah, but what's one more added to the mix? And you know how sexy I think you are when you're pregnant."

"Stop it, Chad." I pushed him away. "I'm not having any more children. End of story."

Then I reached over, turned out the lamp, and put my head on the pillow. Chad sighed disappointedly behind me while I pretended to be asleep.

# Chapter 20

They were supposed to have met for lunch. Kristen had waited for an hour at their favorite restaurant downtown. Then, when her friend didn't show up, this strange sensation spread inside her, the feeling that something was wrong. Kristen wondered if she could have simply forgotten and drove to her friend's house and parked on the street. She sighed, annoyed. They had been friends forever, and never had she stood her up. And when she didn't answer her phone, Kristen got concerned.

She was probably just paranoid, but there was no harm in checking, right?

"Hello?" she said and rang the doorbell.

When there was no answer, she knocked.

"Hello?"

Kristen grabbed the handle and turned it. The door was unlocked. Kristen wrinkled her forehead since she didn't believe her friend was usually so careless. This didn't feel right.

"Hello? It's Kristen; are you in here?"

Kristen stepped inside just as a fly flew at her, and she swiped it away. She smacked it against the wall with her hand, and it fell to the carpet below. A second later, another came at her, and soon she was swiping buzzing flies away using both hands.

"What on earth?"

Fighting off the flies, she soon noticed something else. Something that had her immediately stop and then caused her heart to drop.

There was a smell. A God-awful stench that filled her nostrils and made her gag. Kristen held her nose and fought the urge.

"What is this?" she mumbled.

But Kristen knew what it was. Deep down, she knew perfectly well. Kristen loved to watch crime shows and was very well aware that a dead body, immediately after death occurred, released various gasses with more than thirty different chemical compounds. The gasses and compounds produced in a decomposing body emitted distinct odors; several of them had very recognizable smells, including rotting flesh.

And that was exactly what she smelled right now. In fact, she smelled it so strongly that her eyes started watering the closer she came to the kitchen. The steps she took slowed. Tears sprang to her eyes, not just because of the strong smell but also from the dread she felt.

*Oh, dear God, please, don't let it be true. Please.*

Kristen had a grandmother who had once fallen in her home and laid on the kitchen floor for twenty hours before she was found. Kristen had been the one to find her when she came to visit the next day, but then the smell had been different. Her grandmother hadn't been able to get up and had peed all over herself and defecated.

But her grandmother was still alive.

This stench was so different from that day, and it made Kristen sob heavily already before she saw her friend lying on the kitchen floor. First, she spotted her legs; she recognized the red sneakers that she had envied so much when she bought them, sticking out behind the counter. Then, as she came closer, she saw the rest of her, and finally the pool of blood.

# Chapter 21

"Did you hear they found a body on Cathedral Avenue?"
I looked up from my screen. My colleague, Tommy Harper, stood by my cubicle, looking down at me, a cup of steaming hot coffee in his hand.

I shrugged. "Yeah, I saw it. Why?"

He sipped his cup, and it left the tip of his mustache soaked. "I just thought it might interest you."

I wrinkled my nose. "Why?"

"Aren't you working on the Woods case?"

"Yes."

He lifted his eyebrows. "Then I think you might want to get down there."

I stared at him. What had I missed here?

"I don't understand."

"The woman they found dead in the house," he added. He paused for effect. It annoyed me.

"Yes? What about her?"

He sipped his coffee first before continuing. "She was a witness in the case back then. A pretty important one. She later moved across town."

69

My eyes grew wide. Why hadn't I seen this?

"Shoot!" I said and rose to my feet.

Tommy sipped his coffee again. "Relax. You're new on the job. It could happen to any of us. I'm glad I could help."

He left, winking at me, and I wanted to scream. I couldn't stand the way he looked at me like he was superior to me.

I grabbed my purse and car keys, then rushed out the door. I drove across town, grumbling angrily at myself for not realizing the connection sooner. Hopefully, the local police hadn't destroyed it for me. If this was linked to Woods' case, which I had a feeling it was, then every little detail could prove to be vital in finding the connection. If the local forensics didn't know what to look for, then it could all fall apart.

I sped up and drove through a yellow light when my phone rang. It was Chad. I picked it up.

"Hey, baby. I'm on my way to a crime scene. What's going on?"

He went quiet. "Nothing, if you're busy, then…."

"No, no, I'm driving there now. I have time to chat. What's up?"

"I was just…well, I have an out-of-town meeting again tomorrow night, and I might be home late. I was just wondering if you could pick up the girls?"

I went silent as I drove up Cathedral Avenue and saw the massive amount of police cars and forensic vans. A group of people had gathered around the area and were pointing and discussing, only held back by the yellow police tape. I slowed down, then stopped.

"Are you there? Eva Rae?"

"Yeah, yeah, I'm here."

"Can you take them tomorrow? You said to ask you first from now on."

I exhaled and rubbed my eyes, preparing myself for what I was about to see.

"Yes, yes, of course. I'll make sure to pick them up."

"That's amazing, Eva Rae. They'll be so happy it's their mother for once."

*For once.* That stung.

"Now, don't forget, okay?"

"No, no, of course not. I gotta go now."

I hung up, feeling heavy at heart. Was I ever going to get rid of this nagging guilt?

Probably not. It had been my companion since childhood when I believed I was at fault for my sister's kidnapping. I was beginning to think I deliberately put myself in situations where it became dominant.

Did I like it because it felt familiar?

# Chapter 22

"What have we got? Fill me in."

Detective Brown signaled for me to follow him into the kitchen, where the crime scene techs in their suits were still working on securing evidence and taking pictures and video of the body. She was still lying on the floor. On the cabinet door next to her was written the word LIAR in what looked like blood.

Seeing the dead body on the floor, along with the strong smell, made me gag, and I had to hold my mouth. I found a scarf in my purse that I used to cover my mouth and nose as I knelt next to her.

"Looks like she was stabbed to death," Detective Brown said. "Directly in the heart."

I looked at him. "How many stabs would you assume?"

He glanced at the man standing next to me, who was examining the body.

"Bert? You got anything on that?"

He nodded and looked at me from above his glasses. "Looks like one stab wound straight to the heart. Killed her instantly or at least within thirty seconds."

I could barely breathe as the words fell. My eyes grew wide as I stared at Bert. "And you're sure about this?"

He nodded. "Oh, yes. My guess is it was a hunting knife by the way the wound looks around the edges. I've seen it before and recognized it immediately, but I'll need her on my table to be completely sure."

I exhaled, feeling slightly dizzy. This sounded so much like what Arlene Woods' autopsy had concluded. It could be no coincidence.

"I'm gonna need that confirmed once you do," I said. "And I will need a copy of everything else your people get out of this scene as well." I looked at Brown to make sure he understood.

He nodded.

"I'll see what I can do."

I got up, then took a few steps away from the body, giving the techs space to do their work.

"Care to let us in on why the FBI has taken an interest in this?" Brown asked as we returned to the living room, and I could breathe better. The stench of rotting flesh was still in my nostrils, but with the front door constantly opening to the outside while people walked in and out, there was more clean air coming in, and it made it more bearable.

"Who was she?"

"Her name was Alice Romano," I said.

"Yeah, well, I know that much. But why are you interested in her?"

"She was a witness in a murder case six years ago. A pretty important witness."

He tilted his head. He had nice eyes in a round face. "And this murderer is free again and killing the witnesses or what?"

I bit my cheek. "Not exactly. I think he was wrongfully convicted, and up until now, it was just a theory in my head. But this definitely tells me I might be onto something. I just don't really know what yet."

# Chapter 23

The wind felt strong on her face, and the rain pricked her skin. Mindy narrowed her eyes to see better as she rode her motorcycle across the wet streets, zig-zagging between cars.

She felt her stomach's deep growls but ignored them as she had for hours now. She had been driving for so long, she had almost lost track of time, yet she didn't dare to stop and eat. She had to make it to the state line by nightfall.

She had bought the motorcycle when she and Tuck broke up. He had told her she was crazy for spending all her savings on that monstrous thing and added that she would drive it once, and then it would end up rotting in the garage.

"Life's way too short for motorcycles, or donor-bikes as they also call them," he had said.

But she had chosen not to listen to him, and just to show him, she had ridden the darn thing every day since. She would use it to get to work and back and even go on rides on the weekends and holidays, preferably in the mountains, which was her favorite place to be. It wasn't supposed to, but the thing had become almost a part of her, and she loved driving it even when the rain poured on her face as it did now.

She had left without her helmet or the leather suit she usually wore to ride. But that was a small price to pay. She was still here. She was still alive.

Mindy groaned and felt the pain shoot through her body from when her attacker had pushed her against the counter. But there was no time to feel it or to feel sorry for herself. She had to keep moving if she wanted to stay alive. And that she was determined to do.

Mindy stopped at a red light and breathed, trying to get rid of the fear eating her up from the inside. She thanked God for the self-defense lessons she had taken two years ago when she wanted to empower herself and not have to rely on a man for the rest of her life. They sure had come in handy when she was attacked in her own house. She had kicked the attacker hard and then slammed her fist into their cheek, knocking them out. She had been surprised at her own strength, and it had taken a few seconds before she realized she needed to run. She had rushed to the garage and jumped onto the bike, hearing her attacker get back on their feet and yell after her.

"There's nowhere you can hide, Mindy!"

She hadn't been hiding. Instead, she had fled and kept running. Luckily, she had her wallet in the pocket of her jacket, and that had saved her. She had drawn a ton of cash at an ATM, so no one could track her cards in case they tried. She didn't know quite what she was up against here, but she had a feeling they weren't going to let her get away easily. She had to be smart and think about her every move.

For now, that meant getting out of the state, getting as far away as possible, and right now, her cousin Anne's house in Kentucky was the best answer to that. Mindy had played with her as a child but had not seen her for years. Anne had been excluded from the family many years ago, so her attacker wouldn't know of her existence since they never talked about her. Mindy never knew what happened or what made the family exclude her like that. But for now, that was a perfect place to go.

The light turned green, and Mindy revved the engine, then took off, splashing water onto the sidewalk as she rushed through a huge puddle. She let go with one hand, then felt the pocket of her jacket on the outside, making sure the device was still there. It was strange how such a small thing suddenly could become the most important thing in her life. It's what had gotten her in trouble in the first place, but it would also be the very thing that was going to get her out of it.

# Chapter 24

I was late for my morning meeting. I had been up with Christine several times overnight. She didn't have a fever or seem ill, but she was just awake a lot. I wondered if it could be teething.

I grabbed my files in my arms from the back seat, then slammed the door using my leg and began moving up toward the entrance. I spotted movement out of the corner of my eye but didn't react to it at first. I was focused on getting myself inside and my behind into a chair at the meeting before anyone complained about my absence.

"Is it true that Frank Woods is getting out?"

I stopped in my tracks. Then I turned to look at the guy standing next to me, holding a Dictaphone out toward me. He had a messenger bag slung across his shoulder and wore a leather jacket. He smiled, and I felt sucked in by his bright blue eyes. I almost dropped my files.

"Excuse me?"

He tilted his head slightly, and I felt like a child. I blushed even though I tried really hard not to.

"Alexander Huxley, *Washington Post*. You can call me Alex."

"Don't see why I would," I said.

"You found one of the witnesses, right? Alice Romano? She was murdered in her own home?"

A frown grew between my eyebrows. "How do you know this?"

He shrugged. "Research."

I don't know what it was, but this guy rubbed me the wrong way. I didn't know whether it was the way he looked down at me or the smirk on his face, but something ticked me off. I shook my head.

"I can't comment on an ongoing case."

As the words left my lips, I knew it was a mistake.

"An ongoing case? It has been reopened?" Alex asked. "Because, until now, the FBI has said it wasn't. So, what is it?"

"That's not for me to comment on," I said, trying to sound dismissive enough for him to let me go. I was not used to handling the media, and now I had stepped in it by calling it an ongoing case. I began moving forward, hoping he would leave me alone for the time being, at least.

"I will just quote you, stating that the FBI now calls it an 'ongoing case.'"

I stopped with a deep exhale. "Please, don't do that."

"Why not? Is it wrong?"

This guy was smooth. And I was untrained in this. I wasn't good at lying either, so what was I supposed to do?

"Look, it's very simple," he said, throwing out his hands. "Either the FBI has reopened the case, or they haven't. And with the witness Alice Romano's death, it's pretty easy to think that the first scenario is what we're looking at, am I right? I mean, it would only be natural for you to look at the case again. And I just got off the phone with Woods' lawyer, who says they're going to ask for his release since there is doubt about his client's guilt and since new evidence has surfaced."

"What new evidence?" I asked.

He shrugged. "Those were his words, not mine."

I could feel myself get agitated. Was there something the lawyer knew that I didn't? Or was the journalist just baiting me?

"Huh," I said, staring at Alex. He was really handsome, and I found that even more annoying about him. He was the type who was used to getting everything handed to him all his life whenever he flashed that smile of his or blinked his deep blue eyes.

I shook my head and turned away from him.

"I gotta go. I'm late for a meeting."

I rushed past him and up the stairs, leaving him standing at the foot of them. As I reached the doors, I turned to look at him, and he was still smiling, and then he yelled:

"See you around, gorgeous."

I stared at him, feeling my heart beat fast, then shook my head, even more annoyed with him than earlier, and walked inside.

# Chapter 25

THEN:

It was the longest month of her life. Mary Ellen felt like the days dragged along, and all she had to look forward to was the one call from Ethan she received every day about the same time. He was six hours ahead of her, so it was already afternoon where he was once she got up. That didn't leave them many hours to talk in a day. And he seemed so busy while over there. He kept telling her he had to go because he had a meeting or needed to be somewhere.

It was beyond frustrating.

Not that she ever doubted his devotion to her while he was gone. He kept reassuring her, and he even managed to send her flowers several times a week and would write the kindest emails to her. Plus, he had told her he loved her right when he left, which meant she could think of nothing else but him every day. It helped her get through the day with her job and taking care of four children all alone. When the kids were screaming at one another, she would just dream herself away and into his warm embrace. When the laundry piled up to above her ears, she would think of his bare chest, and it would make her feel so weak in the knees. She'd have to hold onto the washer as she stuffed it with underwear and jeans that were dirty from rolling in the grass. There was nothing better than letting herself fantasize about him, taking her away from the day-to-day problems.

*I love you.*

He had said it, hadn't he? She hadn't heard him wrong, right? Was she making it up?

*I love you.*

He said it, yes, he did, and it had taken her so much by surprise that she hadn't been able to answer it back. It was so early; she wasn't ready yet. He understood that, didn't he?

Was that why he kept rushing away from the phone? Because he was angry that she hadn't said 'I love you' to him? The thought lingered with her for all the time he was gone, and she began to prepare herself for saying it. She felt more and more ready for it, and it was the right thing to do. He needed to know that she felt the same way about him, even if it was fast.

That didn't make it less right.

As she waited for him to show up at her house on the day he returned from his trip, she prepared herself. She practiced saying it to her own reflection as she put on lip-gloss.

"I love you."

She even tried to emphasize it differently.

"I *love* you."

No, that sounded too desperate.

"I love *you*."

She grimaced. That didn't sound right either—like there was a doubt to whom she was speaking when it would just be him in the room.

"*I* love you."

Again, it sounded like there would be doubt about how many people were present. No, there would be no emphasizing, just three simple words, each of them of equal importance.

"I love you."

She smiled at her reflection. Yes, that was it. Keep it simple.

Mary Ellen heard a car and looked outside to see his black Lexus drive up in front of her home. She had sent the kids to stay the night with her mother, even though they thought it was unfair and complained all the way there.

She smiled secretively as the car parked, and he stepped out, holding a huge bouquet of red roses in his hand. He had his white shirt tucked neatly into his black pants and looked so important, the way he strode up toward the door, holding out the flowers.

She opened the door, smiling widely, her heart galloping with joy.

Their eyes met, and as he came up to her, she threw herself into his arms, and their lips met in a kiss.

"Oh, it's so good to have you home. I've missed you so much."

He sighed and looked content. "It feels so good to be back. You have no idea."

"How did it go? You never told me how it went with all your businesses over there?"

His smile froze, and the corners of his mouth turned downward.

"What?" she said and slid out of his arms. "Is something wrong? Did something happen?"

"We need to talk," he said. "Let's go inside."

# Chapter 26

After my meeting ended, Isabella Horne came up to me by the coffee machine while I poured myself the third cup this morning, trying to keep my eyes open. If I put all my hours of sleep together the night before, it wouldn't add up to more than two, maybe three, in total. It wasn't enough to stay completely clear-headed, and I feared I would crash later in the day. I just didn't have time for it. I had three other cases I needed to profile before I could even think about going back to the Woods case.

"We need to have a talk," she said.

I found the sugar and poured some in my cup, then stirred it, hoping it would help me wake up. I took a sip, then followed her to her office, where she closed the door behind her.

"What's going on?"

She pointed at a chair, and I sat down. I put the cup on her desk. I felt nervous as she sat down in her leather chair, and it squeaked when she rolled it toward her desk.

"I just got off the phone with Woods' lawyer."

I had a feeling where this was heading. "Okay?"

"He said that they want him out."

I swallowed, feeling even more nervous. The journalist had been right; he wasn't baiting me.

"They know we're looking at the case," she continued. "I'm not sure we can keep him much longer. They're asking for an overturn of the conviction. His lawyer sounds a little too confident for my taste. If they can get a judge to do that, well, then he is out of there."

I sipped my coffee and looked up at her. "Would that be so bad? I mean, I believe he is innocent. I don't think he killed Arlene."

She cleared her throat, then folded her hands on her desk.

"And if he isn't?"

I paused, my cup halfway to my lips.

"I mean, it's still a possibility, right?" she continued.

"You know how I feel about him," I said and sipped my cup. "I think someone else killed her, and that person is still out there and has killed before."

She nodded. "I do. I do. But I also know you're young and inexperienced. I felt better when he was still on the inside. This makes me nervous—him getting out before we have made it anywhere on the case."

I nodded in agreement. It made me nervous too, but it was not something I wanted to say. I was the one who had argued for his innocence, so now I had to pretend like I didn't doubt my own judgment.

"Do you know what the new evidence is?"

She stared at me. "I didn't mention that."

"I...I heard it from somewhere else."

She gave me a look, scrutinizing me. "I don't know. They won't say. They're keeping it for the judge. But the lawyer sounded certain it would be enough to get his man out and get the original conviction overturned. It must be substantial."

I nodded. "I see."

"I need you on this case full time," Horne then said. "I'm giving you a team."

My eyes grew wide as I lifted my gaze. "Wh-what?"

She nodded. "Yes. You're the one who knows the most about

this case. The agents working on it back then are no longer here. Give your other cases to someone else in your department. This could end up looking really bad for the bureau, and we need to do damage control. We need to be one step ahead of everyone from now on. So far, we haven't been. But that's what I want from you now. I want you to solve this darn murder for me so we can get the right man on the inside, no matter who he is. This is it, Eva Rae. This is your make it or break it case. We all get one at one point in our careers. This is yours. Don't blow it."

I got up and left her office, feeling flustered. This was a very big responsibility for such a young agent like me, but it was definitely one I believed I could live up to.

It was now or never.

# Part III

## TWO WEEKS LATER

# Chapter 27

I didn't know if I was about to scream with joy or cry. I watched as Frank Woods hugged his lawyer inside the courtroom, and a cheer broke out among the spectators. The judge had just given his verdict, and it had left many of us quite baffled.

Overturned.

That was the word he had used. The conviction was overturned. After six years in jail, Frank Woods was a free man. And now, he walked out the courtroom, smiling from ear to ear, and as the reporters threw themselves at him outside the doors when they were opened, he flashed a victory sign. I stood not too far away and could hear the reporters yelling their questions at him.

"What do you say about the ruling today?"

Frank Woods stopped and looked into the camera in front of him. Flashes went off, and journalists were crawling on top of one another to get to him.

"What do I say? I say that finally, justice has been served."

"You haven't been cleared of the charges; the judge was very adamant about that," one reporter continued. "What do you say to that?"

"You heard my lawyer in there, and the judge agreed. My trial was not fair. My right to due process was violated in the original case."

"Some evidence against my client had been improperly gained," his lawyer took over. "The investigators who interviewed him back then and received his admittance of guilt had told him his statements wouldn't be used in a criminal prosecution."

"You were released because of a technicality?" a reporter asked.

"It is a technicality, but a pretty darn important one, and one that made the court side with him," his lawyer answered. "And then let's not forget the fact that new evidence has come up on one of the original witnesses, who, most unfortunately, is recently deceased."

"And what is that new evidence?" someone asked.

"Well, when they went through the witness Alice Romano's computer during the investigation into her death, they found that she always visited her daughter in Philadelphia for her birthday in September. As they looked back in her records, they found that was also the case on September 27th, when she said she saw my client walking through the neighborhood at six a.m. She couldn't have seen him if she wasn't home. It's as simple as that, and we have to assume she was lying."

"Was that why it said LIAR on the cabinet?" a voice asked. I turned my head to see and recognized Alexander Huxley from the *Washington Post*. He held out his Dictaphone while the lawyer shook his head.

"My client wouldn't know, naturally, as he was incarcerated at the time of her death. You'll have to ask the investigators about that."

"But you must admit; it was quite convenient that she died when she did," he continued unabated. "And that they found this evidence?"

The lawyer gave him a look, then shook his head. "I don't see how that has anything to do with my client, and if you'll excuse me, we have some celebrating to do."

The lawyer grabbed Frank Woods by the elbow and escorted him through the roaring crowd, who were yelling more questions at him until he was finally put in a car, flashing another victory sign with his fingers in the window as the car took off.

I stared at Alexander Huxley and noticed he didn't run with the crowd but stayed behind making notes on his notepad instead. His angle on this story wasn't the same as the others, I realized.

I wondered if he knew something that I didn't, and it had me worried.

# Chapter 28

Mindy sat down with a cup of coffee. Her cousin sat across from her, sitting on the chair backward, leaning her chin on the back of it. She had been there for two weeks now, but it was still hard to talk about.

"Listen," her cousin said. "I know it's not that easy, and I don't expect you to understand."

It wasn't just the way her cousin dressed or the short hair. But what really freaked her out was the deep raspy voice and the facial hair.

*A beard. It's called a beard.*

"I told you that you can ask me anything you want," her cousin continued. "I don't mind answering, even those you think are stupid."

There was also the name. Mindy had grown up knowing her cousin as Anne, but now it was Andrew. Mindy had heard about people being transgender and getting sex changes but had never known someone to do so in real life.

"So... you're like officially a man now?" she asked and sipped her cup.

Andrew, or Andy as he preferred to be called, nodded.

"Yes."

Mindy knew that Anne's parents had thrown her out ten years ago but had no idea this was why.

*He? She? I'm so confused.*

She kept getting it wrong and felt so embarrassed every time. From the day Andrew opened the door, she had been in quite a state of shock. And yet Andy had still invited her in once she explained she was in trouble and needed a place to hide. And just like Mindy, he hadn't asked any questions either. At least not yet. He had gone off to work at the computer software company he worked for, doing stuff Mindy had no idea what was but sounded like he really enjoyed. Meanwhile, Mindy had hidden in his house, worrying how long it would take her attacker to find her. She still had her device in her jacket pocket but didn't really know how to approach things from here.

Should she go to the police? Would they protect her if she did?

"So, do you have like a... thing down there?" she finally found the courage to ask.

Andy burst into a raspy, deep laugh and nodded. "Not yet, but someday, I'll get a transplant if that's what you're referring to. But first, I'm going to have top surgery in a few months to remove my breasts. Does that weird you out?"

She shrugged and looked down into her cup. "No, not at all."

But it did. It totally did. Anne was her mother's sister's daughter, and they had always played together when she came over, sometimes staying the entire weekend. Anne had been younger than Mindy, but they still enjoyed each other's company. She was so sad when her mom told her that Anne had been thrown out of the family, and that was the last her mother ever said about her. That and the fact that she lived in Pikeville, Kentucky now. The only reason Mindy was able to find her—or him—was because he had kept his last name and was listed online as A. Elrod. There weren't many people with that last name.

"But now you understand why I left," he said. "In this town, people only know me as Andrew and never misgender me. I don't have to deal with people staring at me or family members telling me, 'It's just a phase.'"

"No, I totally get that," Mindy said, her cheeks flushing. She was constantly so scared of saying something wrong and accidentally offending him. Still, she had to admit that when she looked into those eyes, she only remembered Anne from her childhood, and it saddened her to have lost her completely.

"I'm still the same," he said as if he had read her mind. "I just look different."

Mindy nodded. "I know. It's just… it takes a little while."

"I understand. You've been here two weeks now, so I just figured it was time we talked, that you had gotten used to seeing me like this by now."

"You're right. It just… well… You know."

He sipped his coffee, then looked at Mindy from over the rim of the cup.

"So, since we've now spoken about me, can we now address the other elephant in the room—you? Are you ever going to tell me what you're doing here?"

# Chapter 29

It was late in the afternoon when Grace from reception called me. Again.

"He's still there."

I sighed. "I don't have time for him."

"He's been waiting all day."

"Can't he talk to someone else? I have so much I need to do."

"I tried, but he says he wants you, only you."

"I can't give him anything; why does he keep coming here for me?"

Grace sighed. "I don't know, Eva Rae, but he's being quite persistent."

I closed my eyes and pinched the bridge of my nose.

"Okay, send him up."

I hung up, then closed my case files before I heard his steps outside my cubicle. He stopped and looked down at me.

"So, this is where you're hiding."

"Mr. Huxley. I've been quite busy all day," I said.

"Alex, please, call me Alex." He looked inside my small cubicle and then at the photos of Chad and my children that I had hung up.

"Not quite as glamourous being an FBI profiler as television likes us to think, huh?"

I shrugged. "I don't need glamour."

"We all need a little comfort at least and privacy."

I exhaled tiredly. "How can I help you?"

"I was just wondering...."

Just as he said the words, my phone vibrated on my desk, and I saw that it was Chad. He had called three times already, but I had been in meetings most of the afternoon.

"I have to take this if you'll excuse me."

"Of course," he said. "Can't keep the hubby waiting."

I stared at him, wondering how he knew it was my husband, then decided it was probably just a lucky guess.

"Hi, babe," I said, picking it up, turning away from Alex and wondering why he remained so close to me so he could listen to everything I said. Had he no boundaries?

"What's going on?"

I spoke with a low voice, hoping to keep some privacy.

"I just wanted to remind you to pick up the kids at preschool today," Chad said.

I looked at my watch. "I still have an hour?"

He went quiet for a few seconds, then said: "I just wanted to make sure you didn't forget."

"Didn't forget?" I said it too loudly and looked up as my eyes met Alex's, then tried to smile to reassure him that everything was okay. He smiled back, and I whispered into the phone.

"Why did you call to remind me? Did you seriously think I'd forget my own children?"

He cleared his throat. "Well, you did last time."

"I did not. I was in a meeting and couldn't leave. I didn't forget. I called your mother and had her pick them up. No one was forgotten."

"Still. They were expecting you to come. It's like you don't even want to be a mother."

"Geez, way to make me feel guilty. If that was your plan, then bravo, you succeeded."

With that, I hung up before saying something I regretted. Nostrils flaring and cheeks blushing, I turned my head and looked up at Alex. For a second, I had completely forgotten he was there. I took in a deep breath.

"Trouble in paradise?" he asked, then shook his head. "None of my business, I know. I'm sorry. That was insensitive of me."

I touched the bridge of my nose.

"Just tell me what you want. Why are you here?"

"I can come back later if...."

"No. My mood is ruined anyway. Spit it out."

# Chapter 30

T HEN:
    "I lost everything."

Mary Ellen stared at Ethan. He had sat down at the dining room table and folded his hands on top of it. He had barely been able to look at her since he walked into her house, and she had feared he was breaking up with her.

"What?"

It wasn't the most sensitive way to answer, but it was all that left her lips at that instant because it wasn't at all what she had expected.

He looked up, and their eyes met. She felt a wave of relief rush through her body and sighed.

"I lost everything," he repeated. "My business, my investments over there."

"In Poland?"

He nodded. "Yes."

A frown grew on her forehead. "But... how? What happened?"

He scoffed, leaned back, and ran both hands through his hair. "I... my half-brother and mother, they... they took everything."

"What? How did that happen?"

He threw out his hands. "I left them in charge of it all, and then… they pushed me out. They tricked me."

She grabbed his hand and held it in hers. "I… I don't understand how that is even possible."

"It's different over there. You wouldn't understand," he said, shaking his head. "It's a mess. But I'm not giving up. I will fight for my rights and will contact a lawyer, but that's a process that is gonna take a long time."

Mary Ellen smiled, then looked into Ethan's eyes.

"Then you will fight, and I will be by your side through it all."

Ethan exhaled, visibly relieved. "Really? You'll still be with me even with this?"

"Of course."

"But this means I have no money. I'll have to sell my car just to get by. I'll be a nobody."

Mary Ellen nodded. "We'll deal with that too. Money isn't important to me. Besides, I have a little put aside. I can probably help you out until you get back on your feet again."

His eyes grew wide. He was so handsome; it made Mary Ellen's heart melt.

"Really? No. I could never take any money from you."

She nodded again. "Of course, you can. We're in this together. This is what people do when they love one another."

"You… you love me?"

Mary Ellen laughed, then pushed him lovingly on the shoulder.

"Yes, you silly. I love you."

She sat back, feeling happy inside. She had finally said it, and it hadn't seemed awkward or forced at all. On the contrary, telling Ethan she loved him felt like the most natural thing in the world.

Because it was true.

# Chapter 31

Stefan stared at the car as it parked on the street in front of his house. He recognized it from a few weeks ago, and his heart dropped. Patricia had warned him that it might happen, that they might come back.

Patricia had told him it would be a good idea to disappear for a little while. This FBI woman had come back several times and had gone through Arlene's and Frank's belongings, and that had made them both nervous.

But he hadn't wanted to go because then he wouldn't get to see the kids anymore. And that was all he had in his joyless existence while waiting for things to get better.

And now, Frank had been released from jail. Stefan had known that once that happened, he was in danger. They had already somehow gotten to Alice, who lived down the street and was killed in her home. He would be next if he weren't careful.

He just couldn't get himself to leave the children. What would he do with himself? How would he make it through the day? They were all he had left of her.

His phone rang, and he picked up.

"You see the car?" Patricia asked.

"Yes. I've seen it."

"This is it. You should go."

"And the children?"

"I'll take care of them. Just like I have for the past six years."

"And when Frank comes for them? How will you handle that? He'll come back and take the kids and the house and everything. It's just a matter of time."

She went quiet. "I know."

She sighed.

"You just make sure to get out of here while there is still time."

"I'll be in touch."

"No. No contact."

Stefan exhaled deeply. "You're right. It's probably best. Take care of them, will you?"

"I'll do my best."

They hung up.

Stefan reacted immediately. With long strides, he walked to the bedroom, put his hand inside the safe, and pulled out his gun. He loaded it, then looked at it in his hand, reached inside the closet, and pulled out his weekend bag. He looked inside to make sure it was still packed with enough cash and clothes for him to make it for some time. Then he swung it across his shoulder and glanced out the window at the woman stepping out of the black car. She was short and red-haired and a little chubby, the way women sometimes got after giving birth to more than one child. But not so much that it wasn't cute. Stefan grabbed a piece of gum, put it in his mouth, then chewed while watching her slam the door shut, swinging her purse over her shoulder, and then looking at her watch. She seemed to be in a hurry, and Stefan realized that he was too.

He grabbed his bag, then walked toward the kitchen, and, as he heard the doorbell ring, he went out the back door, slamming the screen door shut after him, then took off running.

# Chapter 32

I know I was cutting it too close for comfort, but I had to do it. I couldn't get the thought out of my mind after talking to Alex Huxley. I still had half an hour before I had to pick up the kids, and this shouldn't take that long. Besides, it was on the way. I wasn't going out of my way to do this.

*I'll make it. Of course, I will.*

I stopped the car, then grabbed my purse and got out. The house where Stefan Mark lived was right across the street from where Frank and Arlene had lived and where her sister Patricia lived with their children now. I glared at the house in front of me, then turned to look at the Woods' house and the swing set in the front yard. In the reports, Stefan was the other witness who said he had seen Frank Woods come home at six o'clock in the morning on the night Arlene died. The way the house was located made it very plausible that Stefan Mark would have noticed him. According to his statement, Stefan Mark had been drinking his morning coffee and looked out the kitchen window when he saw Frank come walking. He looked like he had "met a tornado," and it had puzzled the neighbor. He wondered if they had been in a fight or if there had been something with the kids, then watched him as he walked up to the house and went inside. He hadn't thought more of it until he heard about what happened to Arlene. He had been shocked to learn of her death. He told the police what he had seen right away. Since it was so like Alice Romano's statement, the woman living only a few houses down the street, the investigators had concluded that it was a very credible statement. The two witness statements were vital in the general attorney's case against Frank Woods. But now, one of the witnesses had died, and they had proof that she had lied. She wasn't even home on the day Arlene was killed.

So that's what Alex asked me about. If one lied, then what about the other? Were we going to ask him about it again?

"Of course, I am," I had said, refusing to admit that I had not thought about it yet, to be honest. I felt like an idiot for not having come up with it sooner. This was the type of thing I should have thought about.

"As a matter of fact, I'm going there now to ask him about it," I had said, my voice cracking. I could only pray he didn't notice how badly I was lying.

So that was why I had to go right away and couldn't wait until the next day. Because Alex was going to call me and ask me about it later, he said. For his article. He needed a quote from me on that part. I couldn't risk him writing in his article that we hadn't spoken to the other witnesses yet. It wouldn't look good.

I took a deep breath, slammed the car door shut, then walked up toward the house, closing the small gate on the white picket fence behind me. I passed a couple of garden gnomes on the way to the front door that stared at me like I was interrupting them in something important. I wasn't quite sure what I was expecting to get out of this visit. Did I want him to admit he had lied? Or did I want him to have told the truth and Frank to be guilty after all?

I wasn't sure anymore.

I still held onto the belief that Frank Woods didn't fit the profile of Arlene's killer. But he still rubbed me the wrong way. Everything about this case rubbed me the wrong way, to be honest.

I found the doorbell and pressed it just as I heard a door slam shut in the back.

# Chapter 33

I put my hand on the handle of my gun in the holster, then hurried around the side of the house. As I turned the corner, I saw a shadow rush across the lawn, a black sports bag slung over his shoulder.

"FBI, stop!" I yelled.

He paused as he reached the fence to the neighboring house. He turned his head and looked directly at me. I ran toward him, then saw the gun in his hand when he lifted it and pointed it at me.

I stopped.

"Don't come closer."

I stared down the barrel of his gun, frozen, my heart racing in my chest. My hand let go of the handle of my gun, and I lifted both hands in the air.

"I'm just here to talk," I said.

His dark eyes glistened in anger, and he shook his head. "I have nothing to talk to you about."

"I think you do," I said, trying to sound calm and reassuring and not as agitated and scared as I felt. "I think you have a lot to tell me about Frank Woods and your testimony from back then."

"I know what this is about," he hissed. "Don't patronize me. And don't come any closer, or I swear, I will fire my gun."

I took a step back. I had no doubt that he meant it. His hand holding the gun was shaking.

"No one is accusing you of anything. I just wanted to hear your version one more time," I continued, trying to talk to his sensible side. "For all I know, you didn't do anything wrong."

"You're darn right I didn't do anything wrong," he said, spitting in anger. "I'm not the one you should be after."

"Okay, then let's talk about that. I'm not after you. I'm only trying to talk. Can we do that? Can we please just talk about what happened? Maybe you know something that can help us?"

He bit his lip. Then he shook his head in disbelief.

"You idiots let him go. You let the bastard out. You just let him go. You have no idea what you have done."

"Now, let's get one thing straight," I said, trying to hide how bad my voice was shaking. "I didn't do anything. I'm not the one who got him out. His lawyer is. I'm just trying to find out the truth of what really happened back then. He was let out because of a technical detail and because they found out that one of the witnesses had lied. That's why I'm here. Alice Romano said she saw him on that morning walk past her house, same as you did. But she wasn't home that day, so she couldn't have seen it. She must have lied. Maybe you can clear things up for me?"

He stared at me, and I could tell he was contemplating what to do. I hoped to be able to speak to his common sense. He was obviously terrified. But what was he afraid of?

"Just... let's talk," I said and took a step forward.

He shook his head, lifted the gun slightly, and fired.

# Chapter 34

Mindy studied her cousin's face tensely. She strained to read him, her heart pounding hard in her chest.

"What do you mean you can't tell me?" Andrew asked.

She had hoped he'd leave it alone, but of course, he asked questions. She would have done the same.

"You're staying here with me; I think I deserve to know what you're running from," he continued.

"I know, and I really want to tell you, but I'm afraid I can't. I don't want you getting involved. The less you know, the better."

He stared at her, mouth gaping. "Are you for real right now? You sound like you're a spy or something."

"I'm not. I promise," she said. "But I don't want you to get involved. Can we leave it at that?"

Andrew gave her another look, then finished his cup. "All right. I just need to know one thing."

He put the cup down. Mindy nodded.

"And what's that?"

"Are you involved in anything illegal? Because I can't have that in my house," he said sternly. "I'm not getting myself involved in anything illegal. I hope we're absolutely clear on that."

Mindy looked into her cup, her fingers tapping on the side.

"Mindy? Please tell me you're not involved in anything illegal."

She swallowed and didn't look up.

"Mindy?"

She lifted her gaze. "Define illegal."

Mindy bit her lip nervously. Andy slammed the palm of his hand into the table and pushed his chair back.

"I knew it."

She got up. "No. It's not like you think."

He threw out his arms. "Then what is it? Why can't you tell me?"

Mindy took a deep breath and shook her head.

"I… I just can't."

Andrew ran a hand through his short hair with a deep exhale. "Then I guess I see no other way than…."

She nodded. "You don't need to say anything else. I'll be gone in the morning. Just give me some time to figure out where I'll go."

"I'm sorry it has to be this way," he said.

"Yeah, well, me too…. I figured you'd…."

Mindy paused as her eyes landed on the TV screen behind Andrew. The news was on, and what she saw made her heart drop instantly. She dropped the cup in her hand, and it fell onto the tiles and shattered. Andrew saw it and turned to look. He stared at the screen for a few seconds, at the guy making victory signs into the camera with a smile, then turned his head to face her.

"That's why you're here? Because of that guy? Frank Woods?"

Mindy felt her body shaking, and Andrew rushed to her, then grabbed her in his arms. The sobs shook her body violently.

"Shhh. It's okay," he said and stroked her hair gently, hugging her. "You can stay here as long as you want. It's okay. Whatever it is, you don't have to tell me. If you never do, then that's okay too."

# Chapter 35

At first, I didn't even feel the pain. You know how, in movies, they have that moment of shock before they realize what has happened? When everything moves in slow motion? That's how it felt. I had never been shot before, and the first thing I did was look at the wound in my arm, unable to fathom what had happened.

Soon, tight pressure emerged in my arm, and then it started to burn like nothing else I had felt before. I stared at the wound and the blood while Stefan Mark exploited the situation and took off, jumping over the fence in front of him. I saw him do it out of the corner of my eye and wanted to yell or scream, or at least something, but nothing happened. Trying to move was absolute agony, and I began to wish I would just pass out.

But it didn't happen.

Instead, my knees caved beneath me, and I sat down in the grass, feeling dizzy at the sight of my blood, cursing myself for not having fired a warning shot at Stefan Mark when I had the chance, when I saw him running, after yelling at him. But I hadn't wanted to scare him. I really didn't think he would shoot me.

*My phone is in the car. How the heck am I going to get out of this mess?*

"Help?" I yelled, hoping a neighbor might hear me. "Help me; I've been shot. Can anyone hear me?"

But no one came to my rescue. I felt panic set in as I realized I was all alone. I stared at the wound on my upper arm. The bullet had hit me right above the elbow, and as I looked at it, I realized it had only grazed me.

But it was bleeding like crazy.

*I need to stop the bleeding.*

I grabbed my sleeve with my one good hand, then ripped it off my shirt. Using my teeth to help, I tied it around the wound and then pulled it tight to create a tourniquet. As I tightened it, I cursed loudly. I panted agitatedly while sweat sprang to my forehead from the pain. I managed to get up on my feet. I stood for a few seconds while the world spun around me, trying to focus, then started to walk back toward the street, panting in pain with every step I took.

I managed to drag myself out to the street as a car came rushing by. I lifted my one good hand to try and stop it.

"Help! Help me!"

But the car rushed right past me, accelerating. As it drove past, I got a look at the driver and realized it was him.

Stefan Mark.

"Oh, no, you don't," I exclaimed, wincing in pain.

Anger rose in me and fueled me to push through the pain. I put my hand in my pocket and pulled out the car keys, then rushed to my car and got in. I dropped the keys on the floor as I was about to put them in the ignition, then said some words I probably shouldn't have before I picked them up, moaning in pain. I managed to get the key in, then turned it.

"Ha!"

Steering with just one hand, I took off. I accelerated down the street, flooring it.

# Chapter 36

The pain was excruciating, yet I refused to give up. I wasn't going to let this guy shoot me and get away with it. I bit down hard on my lip not to cave in under the agony bursting through my body. I took a left where I had seen Stefan Mark turn a few seconds earlier. I spotted his Toyota pick-up truck at the end of the street, slowing down for a stop sign. I wondered if he had seen me when he passed me or if he knew I was on his tail. I floored my Chevrolet, and as he turned right, I followed him, coming up right behind him, ignoring the stop sign. The tension in my arm made me cry out in pain, and I realized the blood had soaked through the homemade tourniquet and my shirt and was gushing down my arm. The wound was deeper than I had thought at first, and it refused to stop bleeding. I wondered for a second how long I would be able to stay conscious.

*Come on. Stay awake, Eva Rae!*

My phone was ringing non-stop from inside my purse, and I wished I had a hand free, so I could grab it and call and ask for back-up, but I only had one usable arm, and I needed it for steering. Even if I let go, I couldn't lean over to grab it without crashing the car. I had to deal with this alone. I wasn't going to let this guy get away.

I managed to pull out my gun from the holster in my belt and held it in the same hand as the wheel. I accelerated, then came up behind him, and the next thing I knew, I was on his side. I lifted my hand holding the gun to make sure he could see that I was armed. Stefan looked at me, and panic erupted on his face. My car was way faster than his truck, so seconds later, I passed him and was in front. I slowed down, blocking his way, hoping that would make him stop, that he would realize this was it for him.

He was done.

"Stop, you idiot!" I yelled into the rearview mirror. "Stop your car!"

Of course, he didn't. Instead, he accelerated and slammed into the back of my car before steering around me, passing me, his engine roaring loudly. I screamed as I heard the loud crash and felt the push in my back and neck. I lost control of the car and ended up steering into the railing, loud screeching noises filling my ears as the car continued scraping along it. I then managed to get myself back onto the road and set after him again. I caught up to him at the top of a hill, then accelerated as I came closer and closer until I slammed my car into the back of his truck. His truck skidded sideways from the push and then rammed into the guardrail, while mine spun around, me hitting the brakes, spinning around until I finally slammed into the side of his truck, and my car came to a sudden stop. At the impact, I hit my face into the wheel and tasted blood in my mouth. Darkness surrounded me, but I was still conscious. At least, I believed I was. I heard sirens and voices and people yelling. I'm also pretty sure an airbag inflated and pushed me back, but that is still blurry to me.

It felt like a dream, like I was in the middle of total chaos, people screaming and yelling and someone pulling my arm. It was an inferno of sounds until, suddenly, it all went completely quiet.

# Chapter 37

THEN:

He moved in. After losing all his money, Ethan had nowhere else to live, so Mary Ellen asked him to come to stay with her and the children.

"It'll be a little much since you're not used to having all these kids around," she said nervously, but he grabbed her hand in his and kissed the top of it, then looked into her eyes and said:

"I love children. Especially yours. It'll be fun; don't worry about it."

Mary Ellen tried not to worry but still felt uneasy. Was he just saying that to be nice? Because he had no other choice? After a few weeks of living together, she realized he hadn't been lying. He was really good with the children, and they didn't seem to mind him being around as much as Mary Ellen had feared. And if she was honest, it was nice to have another set of hands around the house. Being a single mom with four children wasn't the easiest thing. There was always someone crying or being upset, and this way, with the extra help, she could suddenly deal with those things more easily. Just the fact that Ethan took out the trash without her having to tell him to felt beyond heavenly.

She felt selfish for thinking that way, but it was the truth. Another bonus was that now she had another adult to talk to, and her bed was no longer empty at night. Ethan treated her very gently and even got up with the kids on the weekend mornings so she could sleep in.

The only issue between them was the money—the fact that he didn't have any and didn't make any. It didn't bother her initially; it was mostly him who seemed to be annoyed with it.

"I hate that I can't take you out to a nice restaurant every once in a while," he said one day after they had eaten dinner. It was two months later, and he had cooked for the third day in a row, insisting that he did it so she could rest and focus on her work.

He grumbled, annoyed while doing the dishes. She told him he didn't have to do both the cooking and the cleaning, but he insisted. It was like he was trying to make up for the fact that he couldn't contribute financially by doing most of the work around the house. It was cute, she thought. But she felt his struggle. It was like he believed that he wasn't man enough in her eyes if he couldn't provide for her.

"I want to buy you jewelry and smother you in flowers; is that too much to ask?" he said later that same night with a deep sigh.

She hugged him and told him those things didn't matter to her. What mattered was that they were together.

"It'll get better. Just give it time."

"How? Everything is gone."

She kissed him. His lips were soft against hers. He pulled away with a groan.

"What's wrong?" she asked.

He got up, then threw out his arms. "I feel so useless. I should be back there, fighting for my business."

She tilted her head. "In Poland?"

"Yes, I should be talking to lawyers and fighting." He clenched his fists like he was boxing.

"But is that a possibility?" she asked. "Is there a way for you to get it back?"

"Of course, there is. I built the company. They tricked me, but it will take money if I want it back—lots of money for lawyers and traveling, and I don't have that." He rubbed his forehead and sat down in the recliner with an exhale. "It's simply impossible. I don't have that kind of money."

Mary Ellen sat down next to him, then took his hand. "I have some savings. Would that help?"

He shook his head, looking appalled at the very thought. "No. No. No. I am not taking more of your money. It's enough that you pay for everything else in my life. I don't want you involved in this."

She put a hand on his shoulder. "I don't mind, Ethan. If it can help you in any way, I'll be glad to. You can pay me back once you get your business back. It's not like I'm using the money right now anyway. Let me help you out. Please, Ethan. I hate seeing you so miserable."

He stood to his feet. "No, Mary. I am not taking your money, end of discussion."

## Chapter 38

It felt like I had been asleep for weeks. My eyelids were heavy, and I could barely open them as I slowly came back to myself. I blinked a few times, then squinted as reality slowly but most certainly hit me.

Then I tried to sit up.

"The kids!"

Chad was sitting in the room, half-asleep in a chair, and I realized it was the middle of the night. He opened his eyes and looked at me.

"You're awake!"

"The kids," I said, panicking. "I forgot to pick them up."

He approached me and placed a hand on my shoulder. "Calm down."

I stared into his eyes, panting agitatedly. "But where are the kids?"

"They're with my mom. When you didn't pick them up, the preschool called my mom, and she picked them up. They're at her farm now with her while I've been waiting for you to wake up."

My eyes grew wide. "How long have I been out?"

"It's been a day and a half since they brought you in here. I came back as soon as I could."

I looked at my arm; it was heavily bandaged. "I was shot."

Chad smiled, then nodded. "Yes, and in a car accident, apparently. They found you in the car. You were lucky. You had lost a lot of blood."

I grabbed his arm. "The guy? Did they get him?"

He threw out his hands. "How am I supposed to know? No one knows what you were even doing out there."

"They didn't get him? He escaped?"

He shook his head. "I… I don't know. I've been here waiting for you to wake up and scared out of my mind of losing you."

I stared at him. "You're not seriously angry at me for getting shot, are you?

He shook his head. "No! no, of course not. Why would you say that?"

"Yes, you are. Chad, I know you. You're unbelievable."

"I just said I wasn't angry. I was scared," he said, stepping back. "I thought I lost you."

I rolled my eyes at him, then leaned back on my pillow. "Gosh, Chad."

"I said I wasn't. What's wrong with you? Why won't you listen to me? Now, you're just making things up."

I sat up again. My head hurt from the sudden movement. "You're wondering what I was doing there when I was supposed to pick up the kids, aren't you? Why was I somewhere getting shot and in the street following the shooter when that was the time I was supposed to pick them up?"

He shook his head again. "No, not at all."

I scoffed. "Yeah, right. We've been together a long time, Chad. I know that look in your eyes. You can't hide it from me."

He shrugged. "Whatever. You're not gonna believe me anyway, no matter what I say."

He walked away.

"I'm gonna go get a nurse and tell them you're awake."

He left, and I leaned back in the bed, feeling exhausted. While waiting for the nurse to come, I wondered whether Chad really was mad at me or if I was just feeling guilty and taking it out on him.

Maybe it was both.

# Chapter 39

"What on earth were you thinking?"

I tried to smile. I was still in my hospital bed when Isabella Horne walked into my room the next day. I had just eaten some questionable hospital food and felt slightly nauseous. I was in pain but feeling better now. I told the doctor I wanted to go home soon, but he argued they needed to run a few more tests to ensure I hadn't damaged anything vital when crashing the car. I told him I felt fine, and it was only my arm that hurt, but he argued that I hit my head pretty hard, and they wanted to be absolutely sure, so they'd have to keep me for another day.

"If shots are fired, you call for backup. You don't go after him alone. You know better than that."

I swallowed and looked down. She was right.

"And... driving with a bleeding gunshot wound to the arm, are you insane? You could have passed out."

"I didn't, though," I mumbled. She didn't hear me.

"What if you hurt someone? A pedestrian? A happy family visiting our beautiful city? An old lady?"

"Okay, okay, I get it," I said. "I messed up."

She breathed heavily, and her shoulders came down. "Don't let it happen again; you hear me? I put my career on the line for you."

I nodded. "I promise. I'll be more careful."

She sighed and came closer. "We need to know who was driving the truck. When the paramedics arrived, the driver was gone. I assume he was the one who shot you?"

I nodded. "His name is Stefan Mark. He's one of the witnesses in the Woods' case. I went to his house to ask him about his testimony back then, and he ran. I set after him, and then he shot me. I managed to get into my car and follow him and tried to stop him, but then we crashed."

"And then he ran," Isabella said. "Okay. We'll put out a search for him. We've talked to the truck's owner, and she said it was stolen from her driveway that same afternoon, but she didn't see it happen. She just came out, and it was gone. She had left the keys inside."

"Why do people do that?" I sighed.

She shook her head. "Beats me. But don't worry, Eva Rae. We'll find Stefan Mark and put him away for shooting you. He won't be safe anywhere in this city as soon as we put out the search. He's a done man."

I smiled. "Good to hear, and as soon as I'm released from here, I'll be all over him about the Woods' testimony."

She gave me a look. "Oh, no, you won't."

"What?"

"You were shot, Eva Rae. You'll be taking some time off to recover. It's protocol."

My eyes grew wide. "No, you can't do that."

"Oh, yes, we're very much doing that. You need to rest."

"You've got to be kidding me?"

"I am not. You get well, then go home and rest. Meanwhile, we'll find your shooter. But Eva Rae, let it go, will you?"

*Let it go? Let it go?*

Everything was screaming inside of me. I exhaled, annoyed.

"I'll keep you updated on our progress," Horne said and went for the door when I stopped her.

"Wait. Tell me one thing. Did you happen to catch the name of the owner of the truck? The one he stole?"

She narrowed her eyes. "Not that it is any of your business right now since you are officially on leave, but it was Patricia Greenfield. And I know what you're thinking; yes, it was Arlene Woods' sister. Why?"

I shook my head. "No reason. Like you said. I'm taking some time off. I'm letting go of it. This is me letting go."

# Part IV

## ONE WEEK LATER

## Chapter 40

Mindy wiped down the counter after the last customer had left. It was almost two a.m. and closing time at the Riverside Bar. It hadn't been a busy night, but she hadn't been bored either. It was Andrew who had gotten her the job bartending, so she could make some money and take care of herself. He knew the owner of the bar, Billy, and he owed Andy a favor, so he agreed to take her in without any questions asked and pay her cash. It felt good to be out in the world again and actually have a reason to get out of bed. When she was at work, she didn't think so much; having something to do took her mind off things, and that was good. She felt better.

"Closing up now, Tommy," she yelled at the guy sitting at the end of the bar, sleeping with his head on the counter. He was one of the regulars, a poor soul who had lost his wife and son five years ago in a traffic accident and never really moved on since. He came in every day at five after work and drank until he fell asleep, and Mindy woke him up and sent him home. Tommy didn't react, so she went up to him and put a hand on his shoulder.

"Tommy. I need to go home, hon."

Tommy grumbled something that she couldn't make out, then slid down from the chair. She followed him to the door.

"See you tomorrow," she said as he left, and she locked the door behind him. She watched him through the glass as he disappeared down the sidewalk and hoped he was going to make it home okay. He only lived a block away from the bar, so he usually made it home just fine. Still, Mindy couldn't help but worry. Tommy was such a good man who just couldn't get through his grief.

"Poor guy," she mumbled as she turned around to return to the bar counter and finish cleaning up. She felt exhausted and couldn't wait till she got home and crawled in bed. She had been a bartender in her younger years, but now it was like she couldn't really deal with the lack of sleep. It wore her out.

Mindy walked to the back, turned out the bar lights, then grabbed the keys. She grabbed her phone and checked it for messages. Her mom had tried to call again earlier in the evening. She had been at it for the past several days, but Mindy hadn't called her back. She didn't want her to get involved in this and didn't know how to explain where she was or why she had left town.

It was just too complicated.

Besides, her mother wouldn't like the fact that she was living with Andrew, who her very religious family had shut out years ago because of his lifestyle choice. She simply didn't have the energy to deal with all that on top of everything else.

"Sorry, Mom," she whispered as she was about to turn around and leave. But when she lifted her gaze, she met the eyes of someone else in the darkness. A car driving by outside, lighting up the inside of the bar briefly, revealed the face.

Mindy gasped.

"You!"

"Hi, Mindy."

The car passed, and the light disappeared. Mindy felt her heart rate go up as she took off running. A glass shattered, and she could hear steps coming up behind her, moving too fast for her to escape.

Then an arm reached out and grabbed her around the throat. The pull back was so forceful that it stopped her breathing instantly.

# Chapter 41

"**W**ould you stop?"

I was pacing back and forth, and by the look on my mother-in-law's face, it was about to drive her nuts. I paused and stared at Miranda across the kitchen. My kids were playing outside in the yard, and I could watch them through the window. Olivia was on the swing while Christine was sitting in the grass in her warm suit, playing with a small Mickey Mouse figurine, putting him inside a bucket, and then turning it upside down and pouring him back out again. Sometimes, I envied the simplicity of a two-year-old's life.

"Sit down, for crying out loud; you're supposed to rest," Miranda said. "You know… get well."

"But I feel fine," I said with a deep sigh. My right arm was still in a sling, but it was healing really nicely.

Miranda tilted her head. "I agreed to take you and the kids in so you could rest, remember? Get away a little. You haven't rested at all since you got here."

I sighed and threw myself in a chair. "I'm sorry. You've been so good to the girls and me. It's just… I can't stop worrying…."

Miranda poured me a glass of iced tea and served it to me. "Is it that case, the one you were working on when you were shot?"

I drank, then nodded. "Yes, it's driving me crazy."

"I don't know much about what's going on out there since I stay away from the news and anything that will make me upset. I stay mostly to myself, and in that way, I remain believing in the good in people and that there is good in the world still. I won't pretend like I understand what you're going through. But I can say this, you're the least rested person I have ever seen, and you've been here about a week now. You're making tracks in my carpet, and I love that darn old carpet. It's been with me since my mother died."

"I'm sorry," I said.

"But tell me," she said and sat down next to me with her glass in her hand. "Why is this eating at you so much?"

"It's just... well, there are a lot of things that don't add up. I keep wondering about Arlene Woods, the woman that was killed six years ago, whose body was found inside a car when it crashed into a tree. I can't stop thinking about her. She was just an average mom; why would she leave her house in the middle of the night? And now we found out that at least one of the witnesses that said they saw her husband come home early in the morning was, in fact, lying. And when I tried to get to the other witness and confront him about it, he shot at me and ran. Plus, I found these books with inscriptions in them from someone warning Arlene about 'the man she was seeing,' telling her to be careful."

"You think she had a lover? That she went to see him that night, and then someone killed her?" Miranda asked.

"Yes... she did have a lover. They were going through a divorce, as far as we know. Frank had found out she was having an affair. He had a motive. I just don't think that's a very good motive."

"But her going to see her lover would be, right?" Miranda said. "Maybe he wanted to stop her? I mean, people do crazy stuff out of jealousy."

"But that's the thing. It doesn't look like it. Arlene was already dead at the time of the crash. Gasoline inside the cabin shows us this person was trying to get rid of the body by making it look like an accident. It has no traits of being a jealousy murder. It's too calculated and planned. If only I understood why the neighbor tried to run."

"Maybe he knows something?" Miranda asked, turning the ice in her glass. "Maybe he was scared?"

"I've been thinking about that as well," I said. "But I can't figure out who killed the other witness. Who killed Alice Romano? It can't be Stefan Mark, the neighbor. He must have known that would only help Frank Woods—that we'd start asking questions. He had no reason to want her dead."

"And you think she was killed by the same person who murdered Arlene Woods six years ago?"

"It's the same MO. One stab to the heart with a hunting knife. You have to be pretty skilled and know exactly where to stab. Most people would stab several times to be certain of death. This person is a trained killer if you ask me."

I rubbed my chin with my good hand, shaking my head. "It's keeping me awake at night, knowing the killer is still out there."

"And they haven't found that Stefan Mark yet? The neighbor who shot you?" Miranda said.

I shook my head. "They say it's like he vanished from the face of the earth."

I grabbed the newspaper from the table and threw it in her lap, showing her the article I had been reading over and over all morning.

"And now this," I said.

Miranda put on her glasses that she kept around her neck while wearing a T-shirt with the words: SASSY SINCE BIRTH. She read the article and looked at me from over the rims of her glasses.

"What's this?"

"Another of his victims. Look." I pointed at a sentence in the article. "This body was found with one stab to the heart, just one, and found sitting in the front seat of a car—the victim's own car."

Miranda bit her lip. "But this... this was in Kentucky?"

I nodded.

"I'm guessing you think this Stefan Mark is in Kentucky?"

I shrugged. "It's a possibility. If he is our guy."

She sighed and took off her glasses. "And let me guess. Now, you want to go to Kentucky as well?"

I leaned forward. "I just want to go check it out and ask the local detectives a few questions. I'll be back in one—two days at the most. Maybe three. It's a long drive."

She shook her head with a quiet laugh.

"Chad is going to kill me."

I gave her a look and a crooked smile.

"You're thinking he doesn't have to know," she said. "You want me to lie to my son?"

"Not lying *per se*. More like just not telling him everything. Please? He'll tell me not to go. He'll never understand. He doesn't get my desire to solve this, but I can't sleep, I can't eat. Well, that's not entirely true. I eat all this junk because I'm so worried, but I can't function properly if I don't do something. No one else sees this connection, and so he'll just be getting away with killing more people. I can't live with myself if I don't at least try—if I haven't done everything I could. I called Director Horne about it this morning and my supervisor. They pretty much just told me to shut off the phone and get some rest. But I can't rest, knowing what I do."

I breathed agitatedly.

Miranda sighed. She clicked her tongue.

"If you're not back in three days, then I'll call Chad and spill everything; is that a deal? And I do think you need to tell him afterward. You can't have secrets like this from one another. The lying is where it starts. Secrecy and lies are like cancer to a marriage."

I sprang to my feet, then leaned over and kissed her.

"Deal."

"I have a feeling I'm going to regret this," Miranda groaned as I hurried to my room to pack.

# Chapter 42

**T**HEN:
    She was cooking his favorite meal—chicken in a paprika sauce that he had taught her how to make. His mom used to serve it to him when he was a child, and even though he was angry at her and his half-brother for what they had done to him, he still enjoyed it when Mary Ellen made this dish.

Ethan had been out looking for work for months now, going from one job interview to another and not having any luck. Today, he had an interview with an investment firm in town. The salary wasn't quite what he was used to, but he was desperate now. Mary Ellen had seen him grow more and more weary as the days and months passed, and she desperately hoped she would be able to cheer him up.

She was almost certain she could.

She stirred the pot where the chicken soaked in the paprika sauce. It smelled heavenly. Mary Ellen was so excited to serve it to him, and the kids loved it too—usually, that was, but you never knew these days. Their taste buds changed almost daily now, and every evening was a fight with at least one of them who refused to eat.

Mary Ellen put the lid on the pot, then pulled out the plates and set the table for all six of them. She looked at the clock on the microwave. Ethan would be home in a few minutes. She drained the potatoes and mashed them using lots of butter the way Ethan liked it best, then placed the steaming bowl in the center of the table before she went to get the chicken.

She saw Ethan drive up the driveway. He had sold his Lexus and had borrowed her car when going to job interviews. Mary Ellen didn't mind taking the bus to work now and then.

"Kids! Dinner is ready!" she yelled, and seconds later, she heard the sound of footsteps on the stairs and coming from the living room. Her youngest was in the yard, and Mary Ellen went to get her and told her to wash up before eating just as Ethan walked inside. Mary Ellen smiled, but her heart dropped when she saw the seriousness chiseled on his face.

"I didn't get the job, in case anyone is interested," he said.

Mary Ellen walked to him, then kissed him gently. "It's okay, sweetie. There'll be other opportunities."

He nodded and finally smiled. "You're the best; do you know that? Going through all this with me. Most women would have run away screaming."

She chuckled. "Well, I am not most women."

"You sure aren't. What's that I smell? Is it...?"

She nodded. "It is. Come and sit down. We're all ready."

"You're amazing," he said and walked to the table. She put the pot down and removed the lid, causing the strong scent of paprika to spread in the dining room.

"I just hope it's as good as you're used to."

"It smells amazing," he said and sat down.

They all dug in while Mary Ellen disappeared for a few seconds, then returned with an envelope and handed it to him.

"What's that?" he asked with his mouth full.

"Open it."

His eyes grew wide, and he made a funny face. "What have you done? Kids, what is this? Did you put your mother up to this? I wonder what it could be? Maybe it's a coffee machine, huh? I always wanted one."

The kids laughed, and he ripped the envelope open, then paused. He stared at the bills in his hand, then up at her.

"Wh-what is this?"

She sat down next to him. "It's money enough for a ticket to Poland and to pay the fee for the first meeting with your lawyer. You're going, and now that you didn't get the job, I want you to get a ticket for as soon as possible. And I won't take no for an answer. You need this, and we all want you to."

His eyes welled up with tears.

"I... you can't afford this...."

"Yes, I can. I just got a raise at work, and I can spare this money."

He bit his lips. "I can't... I don't know what to... how to...."

"Ah, silly. Don't go all mushy on me now," Mary Ellen said. "Eat your food, and then go to Poland and reclaim your business."

"Gosh, I love you; do you know that? This means so much to me."

She smiled and scooped in a forkful of mashed potato and chicken. "Yeah. I know; I am kind of awesome."

"I still really wanted it to be a coffee machine, but I guess that'll have to wait, huh, kids?" Ethan said and winked at the children.

Then, they all laughed.

# Chapter 43

The drive to Pikeville, Kentucky was seven and a half hours, and with traffic, along with my many stops to eat, get coffee, and fill up on snacks, it took about nine hours before I landed in the small town.

I drove directly to the Kentucky State Police Department. It was an ugly gray concrete building outside the otherwise small, charming town—right by the local Walmart Supercenter and Lowe's.

I stopped the engine, then grabbed my coffee and finished it, feeling my stomach rumble loudly. I had left early in the morning, so it was late in the afternoon now, and I hoped the detectives in charge of this case hadn't gone home yet.

I got out, dragging bags of junk food wrappers and empty soda cups with me out on the ground. I gathered them and threw them back inside by my feet, then slammed the door shut, reminding myself to clean it out later.

"A long drive, I take it?"

I turned to face Alex Huxley. He was standing tall in front of me, his messenger bag slung over his shoulder, looking like he just came from inside.

"What are you doing here?" I asked, annoyed. I corrected my bangs and hoped I looked okay, and not like I had just spent nine hours inside my car, filling up on junk. It's safe to say I didn't feel very attractive. And there he was, looking like he just stepped out of a magazine ad for shaving cream.

"I'm thinking... same as you."

"But... how... why?"

Alex smiled. "Victim was from D.C. and... well, there was some familiarity in the MO, so I had to take a look for myself."

"I'll be...."

"You're not the only one who can add and subtract around here, Eva Rae."

I really thought I was.

"No, no, of course. Well done."

He laughed. "And I can't believe that I beat you to it. But say... I didn't know you were back to work?"

His eyes glanced down at my arm. I had taken the sling off, but the wound was still bandaged. Not that he could tell since I was wearing a long-sleeved hoodie. But, of course, he knew. He had written about me getting shot in the paper, and I had read it with much annoyance. It was nobody's business that I had been stupid enough to get shot.

"I don't think that's any of your business," I said with a forced smile.

"Of course not. Did they ever find the guy who shot you?"

"I should go," I said and pointed toward the front entrance.

"Naturally. I'll leave you to it, but I'm in town for a few days, covering the case for the *Post*. Maybe you want to grab a beer at some point?"

"I wouldn't count on it," I said and walked past him.

"Hey, it was just a friendly suggestion," he said, then raised his arms, resigned.

I felt his eyes on me, following my every move as I walked up to the entrance, and fought the urge to turn and look at him, then pushed the door open and went inside.

# Chapter 44

"You lucked out. I was just about to leave for the day."

Detective Murphy looked up from his computer screen as I came up to his desk. The lady at the front desk had told me where to find him. Murphy looked at his watch with a deep sigh.

"Tracy said you were FBI?"

I nodded, hoping he wouldn't realize I was blushing because I was supposed to be at home getting well, but they didn't have to know that. I still had my badge.

"Why would the FBI be interested in this murder?"

"It's just a hunch for now."

He gave me a look. "Hmm, I just had to tell a journalist to get the heck out of here. He had that same look on his face that you do."

I shrugged. "I can't really get into the details yet, but if I could take a look at the fi...."

He nodded, then reached over and grabbed a box and handed it to me. "Here. Knock yourself out. Feel free to use my workspace and computer. I'm going home to the wife before there are no more pork chops left. Those teenagers are eating me out of the house these days."

I stared at his beer belly and thought that maybe he wouldn't exactly starve to death just because he missed one meal, then thought about myself and realized I wasn't one to talk. All the junk I had eaten getting here wasn't exactly helping me get rid of the extra pounds I was packing after my second birth.

*And that is also why I don't want another child, Chad. Not only are we struggling to take care of the two we have, but I don't want to add the extra pounds. I used to be so fit and look at me now. I can hardly recognize myself in the mirror anymore. I stopped looking at my reflection for that exact reason; did you know that?*

Murphy grunted something, then passed me, grabbing his hat and keys on the way. I took the box, then sat in Murphy's chair and opened it. Then, I sighed. He had been right. It was filled with files. This was going to take hours to go through, but so be it. If I wanted to find a connection, it had to be in those files. I needed all the details to get to the bottom of my suspicion.

I took the first file out, then opened it, secretively smiling to myself when thinking about Alex and how he had gotten nothing out of his visit. He was smart, and so far, had been ahead of me, but I had better access.

Which also meant he was going to be bugging me for details.

The thought made me roll my eyes while reading through a few pages of the report made by the first officers on the scene. My phone next to me vibrated, but I ignored it until it did it again, and I realized it was Chad calling. The sight of his name on my display made my heart drop. What was I going to do? If I picked up, I'd have to lie, but if I didn't, he'd worry that something was wrong with the children or me, and he'd call his mom. She might not be able actually to lie to him.

I picked it up.

"Ch-Chad? Hi, honey. What's up?"

"Just checking in. How are you feeling?"

"I'm… I'm good, actually. Can't complain. Being treated very well… here."

"Okay, that's good. And the kids?"

"They're… they're just fine. Enjoying hanging with Grandma."

That made him chuckle. "I bet. I really think this was the best solution, you know? For all of you. Good for you to rest but also spend time with the kids. They've missed you."

I cleared my throat nervously. "Yeah, well... I know."

He went quiet. I heard him tap on his computer. He was working. "And who knows, maybe being with them a lot will help you realize how wonderful little children are."

I exhaled and rubbed my forehead. "Chad... I'm not gonna want another child. I already told you."

"Okay, okay, no need to decide right now. Just think about it. It might be a boy this time, and we don't have one of those."

"What is it with you men and having a boy? Aren't girls good enough for you?"

"Of course, they are, I just... I always wanted a boy; that's all."

"Well, I'm not a vending machine where you just order another kid. It might be another girl, and then what will you do? Try once again? I had a friend who did that with her husband, and now she has six girls. I don't want to end up like that. I don't want another child."

He went quiet. I wondered if I had hurt him. But I had to be honest. I couldn't stand the way he kept pressuring me, and it made me want another one even less than before. Just the thought of being pregnant made me feel sick.

"We don't have to decide anything now. We have plenty of time," he said in almost a whisper.

I exhaled and looked at the files in front of me, then said: "I have to go. Christine is crying."

And just like that, I had told a lie. Up until now, I had kept it so that nothing I said was a lie—just me withholding information. But this was a lie to get out of this conversation, but one I feared I'd have to pay for later.

"Okay. Talk to you later? Kiss the girls for me."

"I will," I said, feeling heavy. "They'd come to say hi, but they're busy playing outside right now."

And that was another one. Now, it was like I couldn't stop. One lie took another, and so the ball rolled. It just flew out of me—like lying to my husband was the easiest thing in the world and something I had done often.

I hung up before more lies came. I hated lying to him; it was painful to have to, but somehow, I felt forced to do it. I wondered why I didn't just tell him the truth. I was a grown woman who was able to make my own decisions. What made us lie to the people we loved? Those little lies that Miranda called cancer for the marriage.

Was it to protect them? To protect ourselves?

Or just because we didn't want to fight?

I shook my head, then flipped a page in the file, forcing myself to stop thinking about it. Soon, I forgot everything about Chad, the kids, and the lies I had just told like it was nothing.

# Chapter 45

I ordered a steak and fries. I know there were probably a lot of things I simply *needed* to try in Kentucky, but it was late, and I was hungry. The restaurant at Hotel Landmark of Pikeville didn't have an extensive menu, and I was pretty much the only one there except for an elderly woman sitting by the door, stirring a cup of coffee. I had chosen the cheapest hotel I could find since I had to pay for this myself.

I had brought my laptop with me and scrolled through news websites while chewing my steak and drinking a glass of Chardonnay. Yes, I know; I know. I should probably have ordered red wine with steak, but Chardonnay was my go-to wine. It didn't matter what I ate.

I didn't see him come up to me until I suddenly heard his voice and spotted a set of legs standing next to my chair.

"Mind if I sit with you? I hate eating alone."

I gave Alex a polite smile. In all honesty, I wanted to say no, but before I opened my mouth, he had already sat down and was looking at the menu.

"How's the steak?" he asked and nodded toward my plate with my half-eaten filet mignon.

"It's actually pretty decent," I said and took another bite. "Fries could be better, though."

"Yeah, it's hard to ruin a steak, right?"

"Quite hard to ruin fries too, yet they somehow managed," I said.

He signaled the waitress to come and ordered a rib-eye for himself. "And a Sam Adams, please."

"Comin' right up, hon," the waitress said, flirting with him so obviously it made me want to roll my eyes. She turned around on her heel with a soft smile and disappeared while Alex sent her one of his charming glances.

Gosh, he annoyed me.

"So, what do you say?" he asked when his beer had arrived and the young girl, smiling widely, had left again.

"About what?"

He tilted his head, giving me a look.

"Oh, the murder case. You know I can't talk to you about that."

He threw out his hands. "You're not even working. You're just using your privilege to get access. Yes, I checked. I called and asked for you, but I was told you were recovering from being hurt in service. You're still on leave, except you're not, are you? Care to explain what you're doing out here?"

I put extra salt on my fries, then dunked one in the ketchup, hoping it would make them taste better.

"I was curious. That's all."

"What was your conclusion today? When seeing the files? It was the same MO, wasn't it?"

I chewed, then wiped my fingers on a napkin and sipped my wine.

"I'll take that as a yes," he said.

His steak arrived, and he smiled at the waitress, then asked for coffee for after with a wink. She left, almost bouncing with cheerfulness. Alex was definitely making her night.

I shook my head slowly.

"Can we be honest with each other?" he asked.

"I don't know; can we?"

139

He leaned forward, giving me one of his smiles. I tried to pretend like it didn't work on me.

"This is the same guy, right? The one who killed Alice Romano. You being here tells me you think so too."

I shrugged.

"But what I wonder is, what is the connection? Between these two murders and Arlene Woods?"

"I'm afraid I can't help you with that," I said.

"I mean, I know that Alice Romano was a witness in the case against Frank Woods, and I see a connection there. But who the heck is Tuck Bowman, and why did he have to die?"

# Chapter 46

**M**indy was gasping for air. It was dark inside the trunk of the car she was in; only a little light came in through cracks and holes every time they passed a lamppost on the street. But worst of all, there was barely any air. She felt dizzy, and her head hurt as she opened her eyes and realized the car was moving.

*How long have I been in here?*

"Help?" she yelled and knocked on the ceiling. She searched for a handle or a string to pull. She knew that many of the newer cars had that in case you were accidentally locked inside the trunk, but this car was old and didn't have one. And worst of all, it was moving, driving pretty fast.

*Where am I being taken?*

She tried to remember what had happened at the bar, and little by little, it came back to her—fragmented, but not that hard to piece together. She had been attacked, and now she was in a trunk.

But where were they going?

Mindy blinked her eyes in the sparse light, trying to see through a crack, but she couldn't really see anything.

What was it they always did in the movies? Something about knocking out one of the back lights? Why hadn't she paid more attention? If she could somehow remove the lamp from the inside? Was that how they did it?

She felt with her hands to see if she could find anything, but it was impossible, and she laid back down with a groan as they drove over a bump and then another one. She jerked up and down a few times until they suddenly came to a complete stop, and the engine was shut off.

Mindy opened her eyes wide when she heard the front door slam shut and, seconds later, the trunk open. A hooded face came into sight in the light from the streetlamp. She couldn't see the eyes of this person or anything else, but she knew who it was, and she didn't need to see.

"What do you want from me?" she asked.

The attacker reached down and grabbed her, then pulled her out, placing a hunting knife on her throat, so close she could feel it on her skin. She gasped, fighting to breathe.

"You know what I'm after," the voice hissed close to her right ear. "Now, find it for me."

"O-okay, just don't hurt me," she said, trembling.

"Walk!" the voice said, and she did. Terrified, she showed the way to the front door of Andrew's house, where she had been staying since she left D.C. It was the only place she had felt safe in a very long time.

She reached the door, and her attacker stayed behind her, knife still in her back. She wondered if her attacker's slight limp was from the last time they had fought at Mindy's house, and she had won. Or at least gotten away. She wondered if she could get out of it this time again? Did she dare to?

"It's... it's in my bedroom in the back," she said as she opened the door and stepped inside, her attacker right behind her, pushing her forward.

"Show me the way."

## Chapter 47

"**D**o you see the connection?"

Alex leaned his elbows on the table. His second beer was half empty, and his eyes were looking a little glassy. He had been talking about Tuck Bowman and everything he knew about him. How he had a girlfriend, that he was an auto mechanic, that he had no family or relations in Kentucky, so it made no sense that he would be there unless the killer took him across the state line, trying to hide the body. But why not bury it? Why place it in his truck in a rest area?

"I mean, why him of all the people? The MO reminds me, of course, of what happened to Alice Romano and Arlene Woods. I mean, that's why we're both here. But who is this guy, Tuck? He doesn't appear as a witness in the case against Frank Woods like Alice Romano did. So, why did he have to die?"

I sipped my wine and picked at my fries even though I had stopped eating. I couldn't help myself; I loved fries, bad or not. I could live off wine and fries and nothing else.

"That's a good question," I said, chewing.

He gave me an intense look. "You know something, don't you?"

I chortled and picked up another one and dunked it in the ketchup, promising myself it was the last one.

"I knew it. You do."

I shook my head and wiped my fingers on the napkin. "I really don't."

He drank from his beer, looking at me from the corner of his eye. "I don't believe you. You're hiding something. I can tell."

I kept eating, my eyes avoiding his, and he kept looking at me.

"Come on; you can tell me."

"Tell you what?"

"The connection. Between the two murders."

I shrugged and picked up another fry, telling myself that this was definitely the last one. I drowned it in ketchup and ate it while looking at Alex.

"Dang it. I won't tell who my source is. I can just write 'a source from inside the FBI tells me,' or maybe just say 'a source close to the investigation,' if you don't want me to reveal the FBI's involvement. I have my ways of covering up. Come on. Just tell me. Please?"

I laughed and sipped my Chardonnay. I was hiding something from him, but it wasn't the connection. I hadn't found the link yet. But I did enjoy messing with him, making him believe I did. It was fun to see him writhe in his chair like this. It made my day. I kept smiling secretively just to annoy him.

"Oh, you're killing me here. Somewhere in this, there is a story. A really good one and I want to write it."

I shrugged again. "I'm sorry. I can't help you."

He pointed his finger at me. "I will get it out of you—your little secret there. I will somehow get it out of you."

"I'm sure you will," I said and reached out for another fry, the very last one, and ate it. Then, I grabbed my purse and put it over my shoulder.

"It's late; I'm turning in now."

"I will get it out of you somehow, Eva Rae," he yelled after me as I walked away, my phone vibrating in my pocket. I put it against my ear as I left him, smiling.

"Eva Rae? It's Rachel from research. You asked for background on a Tuck Bowman?"

"Yes, you got something for me?" I asked and looked at my watch. "Wow. You move fast and work late."

"Well, I like to work at night when everyone else is asleep. I'm sending you the info in an email now. By the way, I didn't know you were back?"

"Let's just say the rumors of my sickness are highly overrated," I said, thanked her, and hung up.

# Chapter 48

THEN:

Being alone with the kids again was harder than Mary Ellen had expected. She hadn't realized how much she had come to rely on Ethan being around to help out. Having four kids was tough, and she felt exhausted and very lonely at times. She wondered if it was just because she missed him, or was there something to this feeling growing inside of her that told her something was off between them? He seemed so distant when they spoke, and sometimes, there could be entire days when she didn't hear from him at all.

After four weeks in Poland, he called one day and sounded like he was in distress. She could tell by the tone of his voice.

"What's wrong?" she asked.

"Nothing. Nothing is wrong. I'm just busy; that's all. How are you? How are the children? Are they behaving?"

"Don't change the subject, Ethan. I can tell something is up. I've barely heard from you all week, only a brief email here and there, and then you called on Monday but had to hang up pretty quickly. I know when something is wrong. Please, don't try and spare me. We're in this together, remember?"

He sighed and went quiet for a few seconds before he said: "Yes, I know. I know. I'm just… well, I don't want to worry you."

"Too late. I am worried, especially when you don't tell me anything. That's worse, Ethan," she said.

"It's just…."

"What?"

"You have so much. You're alone with four kids, and your job and all that. I don't want you to feel like you have to baby me too."

That made Mary Ellen smile. Ethan was so considerate; he never wanted to trouble her. That made her care even more for him. But it also made her even more worried about what he was dealing with that he wasn't telling her. It had to be bad if he kept it such a secret.

"As I said, we're in this together, Ethan. It's what's called being in a relationship. And that includes sharing your troubles too."

He chuckled. "Yeah, you're right. I guess I need to get better at that. I've just been alone for so many years; I'm used to taking care of everything myself."

Mary Ellen leaned on the counter, pressing the phone closer to her ear. She had never loved him more than she did at this moment. She had never met a man like Ethan before, and he was almost too good to be true.

"Please, Ethan. Tell me what's going on."

Ethan exhaled again. "All right. I'm… well, I'm running out of money, and I need to pay the lawyer this Friday. I've been trying to get a loan, but no bank wants anything to do with me, so I've tried to get in touch with some men, but… well, their interest rates are really high, and I know that if I don't pay up in time, they'll beat it out of me. But it's the only option I have right now. Either that or winning the lottery, heh."

Mary Ellen stood up straight in her kitchen. She was making waffles for breakfast but had forgotten them, and now they were smoking. She rushed to the waffle iron and opened it. Smoke spread in the kitchen, and she feared the fire alarm would go off, so she opened the window.

"Is that really all it is?" she asked. "Money?"

"Well, it's a pretty big issue for me."

She grabbed a glove and pulled the burnt waffle out, then threw it in the sink and poured water on it. The waffle sizzled.

"I'll transfer the money to you," she said. "I don't want you to get in business with some shady types over there and get yourself in trouble or end up in the hospital. I need you back in one piece. It would be silly not to help you, especially when I have the money from the divorce that I put aside. You can always pay me back once things settle. How much do you need?"

## Chapter 49

Mindy walked cautiously through the hallway in the darkness. She wondered if she could turn on the light but then brushed away that thought. Maybe the darkness could be to her advantage.

She reached the door leading to the bedroom where she stayed, then paused, wondering if she could get her attacker to come close enough, and she could use her elbow to punch her attacker in the stomach, and then she'd move fast and go for the hand holding the knife. She had trained for this in her self-defense class.

But did she dare to?

It was one thing to act on her teacher's promptings. It was something completely different to be in the actual situation and feel the knife in her back. She knew that this person had murdered before.

*You can do it!*

Mindy closed her eyes briefly and calmed her beating heart, then turned the handle, and in the same movement, as she felt the attacker's body come close up behind her, she threw her elbow back as hard as humanly possible.

Her attacker let out a deep groan of pain, then tumbled back.

Meanwhile, Mindy turned around on her heel, lifted her leg, and placed a kick in her attacker's chest. Her attacker flew through the air, hitting the wall behind, then slid to the ground, dropping the knife in their hand onto the floor.

Mindy went for the knife but couldn't see it in the darkness, and as she came up toward it in the corner, her attacker came up behind her, kicking the knife out of her hand as she picked it up. The knife skidded down the hallway across the tiles, and Mindy set off after it when her attacker placed a kick in her back, pushing her forward, knocking the air out of her lungs as she tumbled against the console table.

Mindy fought to breathe and catch her air again, then fell to her knees on the tiles while her attacker went for the knife and picked it up. Her attacker rushed toward her, pulling her by the hair and placing the knife on her throat again. Panting, her attacker said: "Get me the device, and no more tricks!"

The knife cut into the skin on Mindy's throat, and she gasped for air. Fear rushed through her as she realized she had lost the fight. Defeated, Mindy rose to her feet, being pulled up by her attacker, who was panting agitatedly in her ear.

"If you try anything else, I will kill you and look for it myself," the voice said behind her.

"Okay, okay," Mindy gasped. "It's right in here."

Her attacker pushed her toward the door, and she grabbed the handle again, ready to turn it when a shadow sprang out from behind her attacker, and she felt the knife disappear from her throat. Mindy gasped and turned around. In the darkness, it was hard to see anything, but she still was able to see her attacker on the floor with someone on top.

"No! Andrew!"

He threw a punch in the attacker's face, then another, but the attacker reached up a hand and punched him in his throat, hard. It seemed like such a professional and skilled move; it startled Mindy completely.

It was the move of a trained killer.

Andrew gurgled, then fell back, and the attacker pushed him off. He was now fighting to breathe, holding his throat, gurgling loudly.

"No, Andrew, no, please," Mindy cried.

Mindy clasped her mouth and screamed as her eyes met those of the attacker through the darkness, and the shadowy body leaped for her.

# Chapter 50

"*I can't believe he's dead. Please, send someone. Please. I can't... I can't deal with more....*"

The voice on the recording was desperate, and the woman panted so agitatedly into the phone that it was hard to make out the words. After the last pause, the phone was hung up just as the dispatch asked for her name and phone number. All she had given was the address of where she was.

I nodded at the woman running the recordings and asked her to stop it there, then wrote on my notepad. Then, I looked at Detective Murphy sitting next to me.

"The call came in at three twenty in the morning," he said. "They sent out a patrol and found Tuck Bowman's body in a rest area outside of town, sitting inside his truck, a stab wound to his heart."

"And the woman on the tape? Who is she?" I asked. "How did she find him?"

Murphy shrugged. "We don't know. She was gone when our people got there, and all they found was the truck with the guy inside."

"Couldn't you track her phone?" I asked.

He shook his head. "Tried that. Turned out that the call was made from the victim's own phone."

I lifted an eyebrow. "Really? That's kind of odd, don't you think?"

He shrugged again. "Maybe her own was out of battery. It was quite late, and she might have been drinking and not wanted us to know, you know?"

I nodded. "I definitely think she didn't want to be found; that's for sure. Any prints from the phone?"

He shook his head. "Nothing usable."

"Do we have any cameras out at that rest area?"

Murphy laughed. "This ain't D.C."

"Well, I know that much," I said, then signaled at the woman by the computer. "Could you run it for me again?"

She did, and I listened intently. There was something about this call that gave me the creeps. Was this woman the murderer? Could she have killed Tuck Bowman and then called it in? But why do that? Could she just be an innocent passerby who had stopped her car for some other reason, then discovered the body? Maybe had a little too much to drink and didn't want to get in trouble?

Or was this woman meeting him there?

Why did she say *I can't deal with more*? What did she mean by that? More of what exactly?

Lies?

What I hadn't told Alex was that this killer had once again written a message for us. The word LIAR was written on the dashboard in Tuck's truck, using the victim's blood. It wasn't something the police wanted out in the press, so I didn't tell him, but it definitely linked this murder to the murder of Alice Romano. What I couldn't figure out was what it had to do with the death of Arlene Woods.

If only I could figure that out, then I had a feeling I was holding the key to this case. I kept wondering if this was another job done by Stefan Mark, the guy who shot me.

"Could it be Frank Woods getting rid of all witnesses from back then?" Murphy asked once we had listened to the recording again. "Is that the angle you're working on?"

I shook my head and cleared my throat. "It's too obvious. Besides, Tuck doesn't appear as a witness."

Murphy gave me another shrug. "Maybe he is anyway."

I stared at him, blinking.

"Maybe he just never told anyone, but Frank knows he saw him. So now he's getting rid of them all so he won't get locked up again."

I nodded. It was a possibility, but I just didn't quite feel like it was enough. There was a lot more to this story. I was certain of it.

"Can I hear it again?" I asked.

The female officer ran the recording again, and I listened, closing my eyes. When it was done, I opened them and looked at Murphy.

"I've heard this voice before."

His eyes grew wide. "Really?"

"Yes, and I know exactly where."

# Chapter 51

S tefan bit his nails. He had done that a lot lately, and there was barely anything left to bite. In fact, one of his fingers had started to bleed.

*How am I going to get out of this mess?*

He had the TV running in his motel room and saw the news about Tuck Bowman, whose death everyone was speculating about on all the news channels. Was it a hired murder? Did he owe someone money, and they killed him off? Was it coincidental? A sick monster who happened to pass by, killing him in his truck? Or was he meeting someone in the rest area who then killed him off? Was it a drug deal gone wrong? Could it be gang-related?

They had no idea. It was all guesswork.

But Stefan knew and seeing it made him even more nervous for what would come next. Would they come for him here in the motel? There was a search out for him for shooting that FBI lady, and he couldn't go many places without being noticed. He would have to be very careful from now on—even more than he already was.

Yet all he could think about was the children. He couldn't stand the thought that he wasn't going to be able to watch them from his house anymore. He wouldn't see Izzie fall off her bike and cry again or swing high on the swings and squeal in joy. And what about Ben? How he was going to miss seeing him play with their Golden Retriever, Sonja, throwing the frisbee high in the air and the dog leaping for it but never catching it.

Stefan smiled and shook his head at the memory. Those two kids were so innocent and had no way of knowing about the dangerous world they were growing up into. Sometimes, he wished he could protect them against it, just take them in his car and drive them far away, find a cabin somewhere and keep them there for the rest of their lives.

Stefan shook his head.

"I can't let them do it. I simply can't."

He looked at his own reflection in the mirror, his bloodshot eyes, his stubble from not shaving in days, wanting to grow a beard so he wouldn't be so easily recognizable.

*Why don't you do something? You're the only one who can.*

"I can't," he replied angrily to his own reflection. "They'll kill me, or I'll go to jail for kidnapping."

*But you'll have saved the children from a fate worse than death.*

Stefan couldn't argue against that. Once Frank Woods got the kids back, it was only a matter of time. He couldn't bear the thought of them being around that man again. Those people who let him go had no idea what kind of a monster they had just let loose. They thought he was this family man who was wrongfully convicted.

But Stefan knew the truth—the real truth.

Stefan shook his head again. No, he couldn't do that. He simply couldn't. It was too risky.

He lifted his gaze again and met his own eyes in the mirror behind the TV. Then a smile spread—cautiously but surely—across his lips.

"Or could I?"

He looked at the gun in his bag, then thought about Arlene.

*She'd want you to do it. You owe it to her.*

# Chapter 52

T HEN:
    "What do you mean you didn't get anything out of it? You were there for two months, and you spent almost fifty thousand dollars?"

Mary Ellen stared at Ethan with disbelief across the kitchen table. It was Saturday, and Ethan had gotten home the night before. He told her the news in the morning after the kids had left the table to play in the yard.

"I mean, the lawyers did what they could, but nothing came of it," he said.

She looked at him, waiting for more details, but none came.

"Nothing came of it? Just like that? You're giving up?" she asked, appalled. Mary Ellen didn't understand any of this. She had so many questions, and every time she tried to get them answered, he just brushed her off without really giving her any details. It was getting a little old. She had helped him, and he had spent almost all her savings on this matter. The least he could do was to give her a decent explanation.

"Yes, could we just…?" he rubbed his forehead, closing his eyes. She had poured him coffee and made scrambled eggs and bacon for breakfast, showing him how happy she was that he was back. She had expected him to bring her good news. He hadn't been very informative these past months, so she had assumed everything had gone according to plan.

But apparently not.

"Could we just what?" she asked, raising her voice. "Not talk about it?"

He sighed. "Yes, please. I have jet lag. I'm exhausted."

Her eyes grew wide, and she fought to remain calm. "You're exhausted? What the heck is that supposed to mean?"

"It means I'm tired," he said. "Can we talk about this later?"

She scoffed, then drank from her coffee cup, her nostrils flaring in anger.

"What?" he asked. "Are you mad or something?"

She put the cup down, careful not to slam it onto the table. It took all her restraint not to yell.

"Am I mad? You're darn right, I am."

"Excuse me?" he said. "What the heck are you mad about? I'm the one who should be angry here. They stole everything from me."

She slammed the palm of her hand onto the table, and the cup clattered. That got his attention. She spoke through gritted teeth.

"I'm a single mom. I just spent almost fifty thousand of my hard-earned dollars helping you, and you're too tired even to explain why I lost all that money? And you don't understand why I'm angry?"

She could barely believe they were having this conversation. Why wasn't he more upset about this? Why wasn't he telling her how sorry he was for losing the money? Why didn't he care at all? She had spent years saving up that money, investing it the way she had learned at a class she took at the community college. She had made it grow over the years, cautiously, carefully taking care of it, nurturing it, so she'd have it for later use. She had hoped she could spend some on traveling at some point. So, yes, she felt entitled to being angry. She had been proud of her money, and she had plans for it.

And now, it was all gone.

But hearing her raise her voice at him made Ethan rise to his feet. He grabbed the cup, then threw it at her. Mary Ellen bent down just in time to see it hit the wall behind her. Gasping, she turned and looked at him.

"What in the…?"

Then, he sprang for her.

# Chapter 53

"I sent over the files."

I stared at my email on my laptop and found the one she had sent me.

"Thank you, Rachel."

"I have to say that I spoke to my supervisor, and he told me you are not back working yet. I didn't tell him you had asked me about this and the other stuff, but just so you know, I'm risking a lot by doing this."

I smiled into the phone. "I owe you one."

"A big one."

I promised, then hung up. I opened the email and found the sound file that Rachel had sent me. I sipped the glass of Chardonnay that I had brought with me up to the room from the restaurant after dinner. Alex had insisted on eating with me again, trying to pump me for details, asking me about my day, but I had given him nothing. I saw no reason to. I didn't mind the press. They could be helpful from time to time. We had learned that in training —not to shut the door on them in case we needed them to ask the public for help. But I was getting quite good at talking to him without saying anything important. To be honest, it amused me slightly, this little game going on between us. And his interest in me and the flirting, that probably was just a part of the job; it made me feel good about myself.

Was that bad?

I didn't really know. I hadn't felt like this in a very long time with Chad. He never noticed my hair or even my clothes anymore and never complimented me. Was it wrong for a girl to enjoy being complimented?

*Just don't go too far.*

I looked at my watch while waiting for the file to open. My laptop was still thinking about it, showing that annoying icon, the hourglass that I loathed so much.

I wasn't the most patient person in the world, especially not when it came to computers. They just had to work, or they seemed useless to me.

I realized it was late, and Chad hadn't called all day. I had called and said goodnight to the kids, then spent a little time chatting with Miranda, who told me about the shenanigans that my little ones had been up to all day. I was beginning to feel like she actually enjoyed being with them more than she let on.

And I was beginning to really enjoy my mother-in-law.

We had never been close before, but I felt a connection with her through this entire affair that made me feel like she was more on my side than Chad's. But I could be wrong. Still, I was certain she liked me, which made me feel good about myself, even though we were both lying to her son.

That—on the other hand—made me feel awful about myself.

I thought for a second about calling him and asking him about his day, but then my audio file turned up, and I forgot all about Chad instantly. I pressed play and listened carefully. Then, I stopped it and stared at the screen before starting it all over again, just to be completely certain.

After three tries, there was no doubt in my mind.

# Chapter 54

Mindy took off running but wasn't fast enough. Her attacker grabbed her by the neck, then pulled her to the floor forcefully. Mindy hurt her back as she fell and screamed out as her attacker sat on top of her, then grabbed her throat and pressed down so hard with both hands that she could hardly breathe.

Mindy tried to scream but couldn't. Inside her, panic spread as she tried to grab her attacker, tried to push this body sitting on her away, while the fear of running out of air spread rapidly throughout her body.

And just as she was about to give up, she saw Andrew rise behind her, grab the knife from the floor, then rush toward them. Mindy felt her eyes grow wide and could hear herself gurgle, fighting for every breath as her attacker put even more pressure on her throat. She saw small black spots in her vision just as Andrew placed the knife in the attacker's shoulder. Her attacker screamed and let go of Mindy's throat. Mindy rolled to the side and could hear a commotion behind her back while she clasped her throat, gasping for air, breathing through the throbbing pain and the panic in her body from nearly being strangled.

Mindy coughed and gagged but soon managed to catch her

breath. She closed her eyes while focusing on breathing like she was afraid she'd run out of air again. Her heart was hammering in her chest so loud that she feared it would never calm down again.

She could hear them fighting behind her and turned to look. Andrew and her attacker were entangled with each other, fighting over control of the knife. She wanted to get to her feet, to jump onto her attacker's back and help Andrew, but as she tried to get up, she realized she could only make it to her knees before the room started spinning. She had to bend forward, leaning on her palms on the cold tiles in order not to lose consciousness. Meanwhile, Andrew groaned, and she heard a series of hard punches fall. Someone screamed, and she thought it was Andrew. As she looked over, she saw the knife fall to the tiles again, then a hand picked it up, but she was too dizzy to see whose it was and had to close her eyes. When she opened them again, she felt better and managed to sit up straight.

*I have to help Andrew. I have to help him. I can't abandon him like this. He needs me. He needs me. Why am I so weak?*

Finally, she was able to force herself to get up on her feet, and after leaning on the wall next to her for a few seconds, she turned, ready to make her move.

But just as she did, she heard the sound of the knife penetrating flesh. It didn't sound as loud as it did in the movies, more like when Mindy sliced meat for dinner.

It was the most sickening sound in the world.

Mindy opened her eyes wide and gasped. She glared at the two of them, eyes wide, panic erupting.

*What happened?*

They were still entangled with one another, their bodies so close she couldn't see who had been stabbed. They seemed almost frozen, like two ice sculptures carved in the middle of a dance. Blood was dripping down onto the floor, leaving a puddle below them.

And for just a few seconds, it was like everything in this world had stopped.

# Chapter 55

"I t's the same woman."

Murphy looked at me. It was the next day at his office, and I had just played the recording for him. I had barely slept all night as I had been awake pondering this mysterious information but not coming up with a solution that could tie the loose ends together in a manner that made sense.

I nodded. "Exactly. When I heard the recording from the night Tuck Bowman died, I knew I had heard that voice before. It took a little while before I finally remembered where."

His eyes lingered on me. His mouth was slightly gaping like he wasn't sure he truly believed this.

"But... this was six years ago?"

"Yes. This woman called dispatch and reported the crash of Arlene Woods' car against a tree. She gave the address, then said that there was a fire too before she hung up. She was never found. They searched for her but with no luck. The phone was traced to a trash can nearby where it had been abandoned. There were no usable fingerprints on it, unfortunately."

Murphy kept glaring at me, touching his goatee with the tips of his fingers. He leaned forward in his chair.

"You're telling me that the same woman was at both murder scenes? That can't be a coincidence."

"I don't believe so, no."

He leaned back and crossed his arms in front of his chest. "I'll be... do you think she killed them both?"

"But why call it in? Why risk leaving a trace to your person? Why not just leave them?" I asked.

"Maybe it makes it more fun? To play games with us?"

I shook my head. "I don't know. I think it's something else."

"You're the expert. But what's your angle?" he asked.

I shrugged. "I don't know yet, but I do know that the key to solving this lies with this woman. I need to find out who she is."

Murphy sighed deeply. "I can't help you with that, but there is something else that we have been able to find out." He pulled a piece of paper from a file and showed it to me. "The IT department went through Tuck Bowman's phone and found out he was using his GPS when he stopped at the rest area. We were able to get the address of where he was going."

I grabbed the paper and looked at it. Right there, on the middle of the page, was an address, and it was right here in Pikeville.

"This is excellent."

I finished the coffee that I had grabbed when coming in, then put the cup down. "Shall we?"

Murphy got up, then pulled up his pants. He grabbed his hat from the shelf behind him, where he always kept it, then put it on. He walked to the door and held it open for me.

"Ladies first."

# Chapter 56

He was playing a dangerous game. Being back in his neighborhood was either very brave or extremely stupid of him. Stefan didn't have time to figure out which, and it didn't really matter now.

All that mattered was the children.

Stefan was determined on his mission.

He stared at them from inside the car he had stolen. They were playing outside in the cul-de-sac. Ben was riding his bike in circles while Izzie was drawing with chalk on the asphalt. It looked like a huge painting of SpongeBob. Ben was still struggling to keep his balance.

The sight of them made him smile. How he had missed seeing them. Ever since Arlene died, he had felt so helpless. But now, there was finally something he could do for them. For her. He had been a bystander to their fate for way too long, and finally, he was taking action.

It was about time.

He wondered if he should tell Patricia that he was back since she had, after all, helped him escape by giving him her truck. But he didn't know if she was still here or if she had left now that Frank was back. He couldn't imagine that she'd want to stay in the same house as him.

Besides, she'd only try and stop Stefan.

No one could know.

Stefan watched the children playing, then looked at his watch and nodded with satisfaction. He had been watching the children playing outside every afternoon for years and was happy to see that nothing had changed in that regard. It was a Thursday night, and he also knew that Izzie had ballet tonight and wondered if that was still the case.

He waited outside in the car until the clock struck four-thirty and then saw a woman come out of the house and call in the children. He looked at her through his binoculars and realized she could be no more than nineteen, maybe twenty years old.

"I guess someone got himself a nanny," he mumbled. "How convenient."

Fifteen minutes later, the garage door opened, and the car backed out of it. As they passed him, Stefan pretended not to be watching but managed to peek inside the cabin to see that Izzy was sitting in the front seat next to the nanny, wearing her tutu skirt, while Ben was in the back.

Stefan started the car back up, then pulled into the street and followed them downtown, not letting them out of sight for a second. He sat outside the red brick building while they walked in, Izzie tiptoeing inside, warming up. She had always loved ballet and would tiptoe everywhere, even as a young child. With age, she had grown big and wasn't exactly the model ballet dancer, like the other kids in her class were, but she didn't let that discourage her.

Stefan watched the nanny as she grabbed Ben by the hand and walked in with both kids. The class was usually an hour, he remembered. That would give him enough time to get ready to make his move.

This was it. It was now or never.

*Come what may.*

# Chapter 57

N o one opened the door when we rang the doorbell. Murphy opened the screen door and knocked instead. When he touched it, the door opened slightly, and we realized it wasn't locked. Murphy gave me a look, and I put my hand on the grip of my gun in the holster and unbuttoned it to make it easily accessible.

"Hello? This is the Kentucky State Police. May we come in?"

Murphy pushed the door open more, and we both peeked inside.

"Hello?" he repeated. "Is anyone home?"

He sent me a glare when no one answered, and I looked inside through the open door. Then I paused and pulled out my gun.

"There's blood," I said and pointed.

Murphy pulled his gun as well when he saw the blood on the white tiles. His eyes grew dark.

"Police! We're armed, and we're coming in!"

He nodded at me, and I followed him inside, heart throbbing in my throat. Whose blood was it? We knew the house belonged to a guy named Andrew Elrod. The address was the one that Tuck Bowman had plotted into his GPS before leaving D.C., and this was where he was going. We still didn't know why or how it was related, but we hoped this Elrod guy could clarify that for us.

"Clear," Murphy said as he had gone through the living room. I followed him into the hallway where the trail of blood led us, and as we came closer, we saw a set of legs poking out. Murphy approached the body. He knelt next to it, grabbed it by the shoulders, and turned it around.

Then he gasped. I turned away, clasping my mouth, feeling sick to my stomach from the stench and the massive amount of blood.

"Looks like a stab wound," Murphy said, then felt the throat for a pulse, even though we both knew it was in vain. This guy had been dead for days. Murphy shook his head, then rose to his feet while I put my gun back in the holster. I looked around, searching for anything written with the blood, a word, LIAR. But I didn't find anything, and that puzzled me.

"Also looks like this one picked up a fight," I said and nodded toward the console table that had been turned over and two or three picture frames that were shattered. "He didn't go down easily. You might find DNA under his nails if we're lucky."

Murphy stared at the body, then tilted his head. "His shirt is torn here; what's that black thing he's wearing underneath?"

I bent forward to look.

"It's a binder," I said. "It's used to hide breasts. He's not a he, or at least wasn't born a male."

"So, he's like a trans?"

"Transgender," I said, nodding.

"Could it be a hate crime, then?" he asked.

I sighed and ran a hand through my bangs.

"It would be strange, given the circumstances, right? I mean, this is the guy that our other victim was coming to visit. Now, he's dead too?"

Murphy bit his lip.

"Could they have been in a relationship? I'm calling it in now, getting the forensics team out here so we can get some answers. Out here, it can take a while."

Murphy left with the phone clutched against his ear. I stared at the frames on the floor. I recognized our victim in the photos beneath the shattered glass.

It gave me an idea.

"His phone. I need to find this guy's phone," I mumbled to myself, then rushed into a bedroom where I found it next to the bedside, still in the charger.

*Lucky punch.*

"All right, I called it in. We should probably not touch anything," Murphy said, coming back.

I stared at the phone in my hand and knew he was right. Yet I had to try anyway, so I took a chance and tried the password 1234. It worked, much to my surprise, and I opened it. It was surprising how many people didn't protect their stuff properly. It was almost too easy.

"What are you doing?" Murphy asked, coming up behind me. "I don't think we should touch stuff."

I opened the photo app and looked at the last couple of pictures taken with his phone. A lot of them were of him with someone else. There were a lot of them, taken in various places in the town, eating or just goofing around. They seemed close but not like a couple.

And it was a woman.

*Could it be? Could I be this lucky?*

"Who is that?"

"Do you remember how the voice in the nine-one-one recording said, *'I can't deal with more…?'* I kept wondering *more what*? Was it lies? Troubles? But it just occurred to me; she meant *more deaths*. She has seen too many people die."

"You're saying that you believe this is our caller? Both the one from a few days ago and six years ago?"

"With a little luck and a lot of help from above, yes. It could be the woman we're looking for."

Murphy gave me a skeptical look. "Really?"

"Listen, it's all we've got, and I have a hunch about this woman. She's the one we're looking for."

I fiddled with the phone and airdropped the photo of the

woman to my own phone, then looked down at Murphy, handing him the victim's phone.

"So, now, all we need to do is to find her before the killer does," he said. "Isn't that what FBI agents say?"

I nodded on my way out the door. In the distance, I could hear the sirens getting closer. I paused with an exhale.

"They also often add, *If it's not too late.*"

# Part V

ONE WEEK LATER

# Chapter 58

He didn't look like a broken man. If he was, then I could only tell slightly in his appearance. His stubble told a story of not having shaved in a long time, and his hair was messed up like he had just been napping as he let me inside his kitchen, and I sat down. But he was still handsome like he had been inside the prison when I saw him the last time.

"Please, make it brief," Frank Woods said. He didn't sit down but stood by the sink, leaning on the counter behind him.

"You have somewhere to be?"

"No, I'm just... what's this about?"

I found the picture of the woman on my phone, then handed it to him. He took it, even though it was a little reluctant.

"Who is this?"

"Do you recognize her?" I asked.

He looked again, then shook his head. "No. Am I supposed to?"

I bit my lip, trying to read his expression. I was usually pretty good at telling if someone was lying to me, but Frank was harder to read than most people. He had an instant coldness passing like a mask over his face, blotting out all expression, at least for the most part. Now and then, I felt like I could see something in his eyes that made me think he wasn't completely made of stone. But then his face and voice would remain cold and expressionless. It made me wonder whether he cared.

"Her name is Mindy Lynn," I said, hoping to see a reaction on his face, but none came.

"Doesn't ring a bell," he said.

I had gotten the name from the bar where Mindy had been working nights in Pikeville. I had spent days talking to neighbors, asking them about her, and they had told me Mindy showed up recently all of a sudden and that she apparently was Andrew's cousin. They also told me she worked at the bar downtown as a bartender and that she and Andrew seemed very fond of one another. That fit well with the pictures I had seen on his phone. We hadn't found many of her belongings in the house except for some clothes in the bedroom that we assumed she slept in since there were only two bedrooms in the house. No phone or wallet, no personal stuff. I couldn't help but wonder if she had managed to get away or if our killer had her. Every day, I feared I'd wake up and hear of her body turning up somewhere.

"Listen, Frank. This is in your interest too that we find her. She might know something that can keep you out of jail. We think she was the one who called it in on the night Arlene died. She could be a witness. She might have seen someone else get out of the car and set it on fire before leaving. She might have seen the killer. This is in your interest too, Frank, if you want to stay out of jail."

Finally, I saw some sort of expression on his face. It didn't last long, but just long enough for me to see it.

And then it was gone. The stone-cold mask was back.

"I'm sorry. I wish I could help you," he said and handed me back the phone. He tried to smile, but it came off as awkward. "I'm happy to be out of jail; don't get me wrong. I'm with my kids, and that's all that matters."

I exhaled. "Your kids have been missing for a week, Frank."

"Don't you think I know that?" he hissed, finally showing emotion. "But you idiots come here instead of being out there searching for them. I need them back. And now you come here asking me about some woman who may or may not be a witness from six years ago? What about my children? Are you people even looking for them?"

"Well, I'm not on that case, so…."

He threw out his arms. "Of course, you aren't. Why would you be? Why would I assume that's why you came here?"

I nodded. "I'm sorry, Frank. I know they're doing everything they can to search for them."

His eyes flared up, then calmed down again. "I know. It's just so…. He grabbed a cup and threw it against the wall next to him. The handle fell off, but it didn't shatter. "Frustrating."

I got up, putting my phone back in my pocket.

"I'm sorry. I'll leave you now."

I walked out of the kitchen, and as I did, I saw a pile of papers lying on the counter. The one on top grabbed my attention, and I stopped.

"You going somewhere, Frank? These look like airplane confirmations?" I gave him a look. "You're not supposed to leave the state, let alone the country. You have another trial coming up."

"No, these are old," he said as he grabbed the papers and put them behind his back. "They're not even mine. Patricia went on a trip with the kids some months ago. That's not illegal."

I smiled. "Didn't say it was."

He gave me a cool little nod of dismissal as he let me out of the hallway and slammed the door shut behind me.

# Chapter 59

**T**HEN:
    She made it to the bathroom and managed to shut the door and lock it behind her. Panting, Mary Ellen fell to her knees while Ethan turned the handle, then knocked on the door.

"Open up, Mary!"

She breathed heavily, then looked down at her shaking hands. It was the look in Ethan's eyes when he went for her. They had been filled with such anger. She knew she had to make a run for it.

"Mary!"

He was hammering on the door now, and it startled Mary Ellen. Her heart was beating hard in her chest, and she was struggling to breathe.

*What do I do? How do I get out of here?*

Ethan was still hammering on the door when Mary Ellen rose to her feet and walked to the toilet. There was a small window under the ceiling, and by standing on the toilet, she could look out. It couldn't open, but she could look outside.

"Mary! Open the freaking door!"

Ethan was yelling and hammering hard on the door. Mary Ellen whimpered in fear. She looked out the window and could see the kids playing in the yard. Seeing them made her start to cry.

She knocked on the window.

"Kids! Hello?"

Mary Ellen was crying now, yelling the children's names between sobs. She knocked on the window, tears running down her cheeks. But the children didn't hear her. Mary Ellen then spotted her neighbor pulling weeds in her yard.

"Brenda, hello? Brenda? Help!"

Mary Ellen knocked as loudly and forcefully she could while sobbing violently. Outside, Ethan was now hammering both his fists into the door while screaming her name. The sound of his voice, the anger she detected in it, made her shiver in fear. She had never seen him like this before. But she had seen it in the eyes of her own father as a child and knew what it meant. She knew no pleading or begging would calm him. She had grown up listening to her own mother get beaten or simply humiliated for being so stupid, and she had sworn she'd never end up in a relationship like that.

How did it happen anyway?

"Brenda, please? Help me," she said, now slamming the palm of her hand into the window. "Kids? Please?"

But no one reacted. The kids continued playing while Brenda bent down and pulled more weeds, not even lifting her head to look in Mary Ellen's direction.

It was no use.

Crying, Mary Ellen turned to look at the locked door. Ethan had stopped hammering, and the silence was getting to her. What was he up to?

Mary Ellen climbed down from the toilet, then walked to the door to listen, but there was nothing to hear.

*What's he doing?*

Mary Ellen waited for a few minutes with a hand on the door like she believed she could somehow feel through it what was happening on the other side. She breathed agitatedly, her heart refusing to calm down.

179

Then, she decided to open the door. She grabbed the handle and pulled it open.

Nothing.

"E-Ethan?"

She walked out into the hallway and looked to the sides. He wasn't there.

*Where did he go?*

She found him in the living room, sitting in the recliner, hiding his face between his hands. She calmed down and approached him. He didn't seem as dangerous now.

"I'm sorry," he said, speaking through his hands as she came closer. "I'm so so sorry."

Mary Ellen exhaled, relieved. She placed a hand on his arm. He looked at her, pulling his hands aside. He had been crying.

"I don't normally… I don't know what's gotten into me lately. It's all the stress about my business and my… stupid half-brother…. Gosh, I hate him. I'm sorry. I shouldn't be taking it out on you."

Mary Ellen exhaled. She forced a smile. "It's a lot. I get it. It's driving you nuts. It's not so strange."

He sighed and took her face between his hands. "How did I get so lucky to find you? You're the best thing that ever happened to me. I love you so much."

That made her blush. He looked deeply into her eyes while he said the words, and she couldn't help smiling. This was just a misstep. It didn't have to matter to her if she didn't let it. After all, everyone could bend under pressure, right? When things became too much? She had found herself yelling at the children when it wasn't necessary as well. It was just a mistake.

"I hope you can forgive me," he said. "I hope I didn't ruin everything. I am so sorry if I scared you. I really am. It's breaking my heart. Please, don't leave me because of this. I promise it'll never happen again. I don't normally do things like that—let the anger eat me up like that. I honestly don't know what came over me. Can you forgive me? Do you think you can?"

"Of course, I can forgive you," she said. "I love you too. Let's just forget it ever happened, okay?"

She smiled at him, thinking she was lucky to have such a sensitive and wonderful man in her life who was even able to see his own mistakes and ask for forgiveness. Not many men were able to do that. And this was a solo incident; it wouldn't happen again, he said. Besides, he had never done anything like this before, so it would be easy to forget.

Mary Ellen stared into his eyes, then touched his cheek gently while feeling guilt spread inside her stomach, wondering if she had exaggerated things by running into the bathroom. Ethan probably would never have hurt her if she hadn't. She had probably made things worse by assuming he wanted to harm her and locking herself in the bathroom.

"I'm so lucky to have found you," he said and pulled her into a kiss. "I don't know how I would have gone through all this without you, and I don't know what I would do without you. I'd probably kill myself."

# Chapter 60

I sat in my car outside in the cul-de-sac when I saw the garage door open. I had just left Frank Woods and still had this odd feeling inside me that I couldn't escape. Something was off with him.

He had reported the children missing a week ago, so maybe that was just it; I guess that could drive anyone nuts. They had gone to Izzy's ballet class with the nanny on a Thursday afternoon as usual, but the children never returned. Only the nanny did. She had told the police an insane story about someone invading her car when she came back out with the kids. Ben was in the back seat, and she and Izzy had gotten in the front when the door was pulled open, and someone grabbed her by the throat, then pulled her out of the car. The masked man then jumped into the driver's seat and took off seconds later with both kids. They had found no witnesses to the incident, even though it happened in the middle of a busy street, which was puzzling to the investigators. For now, the nanny wasn't being treated as a suspect in the kidnapping case.

When I heard the story, I kept wondering why these kidnappers had chosen this moment and those children. I didn't believe in coincidences. It had to be related to the murder case somehow; maybe it was some crazed guy who had read about Frank Woods being released.

Maybe it was something else.

The media had, of course, thrown themselves at the story and were constantly writing about it; most of it was stuff that just made the FBI look like incompetent fools. Needless to say, Isabella Horne wasn't happy.

Meanwhile, I was back with the girls in our own house, and Chad had no clue what I had been up to in Kentucky. It remained mine and Miranda's secret. Not that I was proud of keeping it a secret, but I just didn't want to deal with him right now. I had, however, promised Miranda that I'd tell him soon, so I was finding the courage to do so.

Just not today.

Then I saw Frank Woods suddenly leave his house, seemingly in a rush. I couldn't help but wonder where he was going. I started the car back up and followed him. He drove into town, then took a left down Shepherd Street and drove into a neighborhood of cute little townhouses.

He stopped in front of one of them. I parked farther down the street and kept a close eye on him as he got out and walked up to the small porch. A woman came out to greet him outside, and they started to talk. Frank's arms gesticulated wildly, and I could tell he was upset. She covered her face with her hands and looked like she was crying. He was yelling now, it was obvious, while she was shaking and sobbing. Then he was about to leave, and she tried to stop him. She shook her head and grabbed him by the shoulders, trying to keep him there. But he pushed her away, then threw out his arms, yelling at her before he walked down the stairs toward the car, shouting something after her. As he took off, she stood behind on the porch, crying, hiding her face again.

I let Frank go, then watched the woman on the porch. As soon as she went back inside and shut the door, I left my car.

# Chapter 61

S he was beyond paranoid. Mindy couldn't remember when she had last slept through the entire night or even felt remotely safe during the day. Well, not since she had been in Andrew's house, and that had turned out not to be a safe place at all. So, now, she trusted no one and moved from place to place every day, never staying in the same motel twice. While working at the bar in Pikeville, she had managed to put a good sum of money aside and kept it all in cash in her bag, so she couldn't be traced. She figured she could live like this for about two months; then she'd run out of money and would have to take another job, probably bartending again.

*But how long can you keep this up? Will you be on the run for the rest of your life?*

Mindy sat by the window of her motel room, looking out at the parking lot and the few cars driving by on the road outside. She stayed like that most nights, constantly keeping an eye on her surroundings, jumping every time a car approached.

And she felt so incredibly tired.

Mindy closed her eyes briefly to rest, giving into that luring sleep that kept calling her, but every time she did, she'd see Andrew's dead body on the floor of his house, and the terror would wake her up.

Mindy gasped and looked outside again. It was raining heavily, and the cars were driving slowly. Meanwhile, the worry in the pit of her stomach threatened to make her panic.

*What am I going to do?*

She had gotten out of the house just in time. Right when she saw Andrew fall to the floor, she had lifted a vase in the hallway and thrown it at her attacker. Then she had run into the bedroom, grabbed her purse with her wallet and everything important, like the device that she knew her attacker wanted, and opened the window and crawled out. She had then run like the wind across all the neighboring yards until she finally came to a street, where she had found a car parked in front of a house with the engine running. She had felt bad for taking it since she knew that someone probably needed it, but it had been her only way out, her only way of surviving. She had driven out of town, thinking she had escaped her attacker when she had passed a rest area and recognized a truck parked there. She had taken the next highway exit, then driven back to the rest area, just to be sure she was wrong.

But she wasn't. It was Tuck's truck, and what she found inside it terrified her to the core. Tuck in a pool of his own blood. Mindy had felt so sick; she had run to the bushes and thrown up. Shaking heavily, she had then opened the passenger door and grabbed his phone from the dashboard, and made the call. She had then wiped off the phone, so they wouldn't find her fingerprints on it or the doorhandle before closing the door again and taking off. She had wanted to tell them about Andrew's body as well, but she had panicked while talking to the woman and hung up mid-sentence. Since then, she had been afraid that the police might track her down too. She feared they'd never believe her if she told them the truth. So now, she wasn't just running from a killer; she was also afraid of ending up in jail.

It was no wonder she felt paranoid.

Mindy sighed deeply and kept staring at the road when a car

turned into the parking lot. Mindy rose to her feet when seeing it, heart throbbing in her chest.

The car parked right outside her window, and seconds later, there was an aggressive knock on her door.

# Chapter 62

"Yes?"

I smiled at the woman in the doorway in front of me, then showed her my badge. "FBI, can I come in?"

She gave me a puzzled look but stepped aside and let me in. I walked past her into the living room. The door to a children's room was left open, and I could see stuffed animals on shelves and toys in containers and boxes. But I saw no children.

The woman crossed her arms in front of her chest. She seemed nervous.

"What is this about?"

"The man who was here just before," I said. "Frank Woods."

"Wh-what about him?"

"How well do you know him?"

She shook her head. "I don't... it's just... I don't really know him at all."

A frown grew between my eyebrows. "You seemed like you knew one another pretty well out there. It actually looked like you were fighting."

"Oh, that... it was nothing... just some issues, mind if I ask why you're asking about him?" she said.

"Well, as you might know, he's got his retrial coming up," I said, scrutinizing her face. She wasn't looking at me anymore. Her eyes hit the floor.

"I wouldn't know anything about that."

"What about his wife?" I asked, and the woman looked up at me, eyes growing wide. "Did you know her?"

"A-Arlene?" she shook her head. "I didn't really... listen—I don't really have time for this. I have to... to...."

"But you knew her?"

She exhaled, sounding exhausted. "I heard about her in the news like most people. Could you please leave? I have to... I need to get going...."

"Listen, if Frank is bothering you, and it looked to me like he was, then please tell me, and I'll make sure he is...."

"Could you please just leave it alone?" the woman hissed at me. "I don't know Frank or Arlene. I just... I just want to be left alone."

I stared at her. Her eyes were flaming with anger and frustration, and I also detected a huge amount of desperation in them. She definitely wasn't being honest with me, and it didn't take a genius to figure that out.

"I'm sorry," I said. "I didn't mean to bother you."

I paused and looked around. Pictures on the wall told me she had four children, two boys and two girls.

"I'm sure you're busy with all those kids," I said and looked at a photo in a frame. "How old are they?"

The woman went quiet and stood like she was frozen, staring at me, then spoke with a small, fragile voice, "I think you should leave now."

## Chapter 63

**T**HEN:
    On the good days, they did better than most couples. On the good days, that was. On the bad ones, it was, well, bad, terrible maybe even, but Mary Ellen tried hard not to focus on that. Ethan had been thrown into a deep depression, and it wasn't his fault that things just wouldn't get better for him. If only she didn't always say the wrong things to set him off. Mary Ellen soon learned not to mention the business, the half-brother, or even money to him. As long as she stayed off those topics, she was fine. Then, he didn't throw plates or coffee cups at her, nor did he yell all night, telling her how stupid she was and how much he felt like a failure already, so she didn't need to rub it in his face.

So, now, they only spoke about those things when he asked for more money. And he did that a lot. He said it was for the lawyers, who were still working on helping him out in Poland. And Mary Ellen had stopped asking for results, or even how it was going. She just transferred the money to his account when he needed it, and when she ran out of her savings, she took an extra job at night wait-ressing to make enough to keep them afloat. Ethan told her he couldn't go out and get a job since he wasn't a citizen, so he had no work permit. This puzzled her because he told her he had been married to an American woman earlier, so she thought he'd automatically become a citizen, but maybe she was wrong. And perhaps it didn't matter. Experience had taught her not to ask about such things. Ethan knew what he was talking about, and he was going to get his money and his business back at some point, he assured her. It was just taking a little longer than he had expected it to.

"And then we'll be rich and can travel the world," he'd tell her on the good days when he was in a good mood. And she'd be so excited about that. Mary Ellen couldn't wait to see the world, even if it took longer than they expected. She didn't mind working the extra shifts to make it happen. It was a small price to pay. And as soon as Ethan succeeded, he would also be in a better mood. She knew he would. They would have less of the bad days, and he would not throw plates and cups around or chase her into the bathroom, hammering on the door anymore. He wouldn't accidentally slap her across the face either and have to apologize again.

That would be history—just a bump in the road.

"We all have bumps we need to get over or through," she'd tell her own reflection while covering up the bruises using concealer. Besides, Ethan was so good with the children. They adored him, and Mary Ellen couldn't bear for them to lose another father figure. Ethan was a good man, and they'd be very happy together soon. Very soon. They just needed to get over this hurdle.

*Soon.*

Mary Ellen stared at her reflection in the mirror before she went to open the door. She had to make sure no one could see that awful big bruise on her cheek from Ethan's ring the other day when she had accidentally asked about her birthday that was coming up, and if he thought they might be able to go out for dinner, so she didn't have to cook.

She smiled when she saw that it was still covered by the thick foundation she had put on this morning when taking the kids to school.

Then she opened the door. Outside stood two men she hadn't seen before. They looked very serious at her, then showed her their badges.

"We need you to come with us to the station, ma'am."

# Chapter 64

"Where have you been?"

Chad was in the living room when I got home. I had picked the girls up from pre-school on my way and thought I would make it back before he was done with his meeting downtown. I put the girls' bags on the floor, then let them run off to play in their room.

"I was just picking up the girls," I said and put my purse down, avoiding looking at him. "How was your meeting?"

He sent me a look. "My meeting was canceled, so I came back home, and guess what I found here? Not you. You're supposed to be resting. You were shot, remember? So, where were you?"

I cleared my throat. "I just had to go talk to this woman."

He exhaled, annoyed. "You were working again? You still have a week until you go back. Why can't you just stay home and relax?"

I sat down with a sigh. "It was just...."

He leaned forward. "You've been working all this time, haven't you?"

My eyes grew wide, and I lifted my gaze. "Your mom told you?"

He shook his head with an exhale. "No, but you just did. Dang it, Eva Rae."

192

He rose to his feet with a groan. He paced back and forth a few times, running a hand through his hair.

"Are we not enough for you? All we asked was that you stayed away from work for a few weeks. Your boss even recommended it. You were shot, Eva Rae. It terrified me. Don't you understand that? I'm scared every time you go to work, fearing I won't get you back home. You need to take better care of yourself. Not only for your own sake but for all of us."

"Oh, come on," I said. "I was just trying out a few different angles. This case is keeping me awake at night. We found two more victims in Kentucky, and I had to look into that. And today, I went to visit this woman who...."

"Kentucky? You went out of state and didn't even tell me?" Chad stared at me like he couldn't believe I had just said that. I bit my lip, thinking this wasn't the right moment to tell him, but would that time ever come? I had promised his mom I'd tell him at some point, and now, I guess I had.

"Yes, well..."

He threw out his arms. "When was that?"

"Wh-when I stayed at your mom's?"

"You left the children and went out of state to look for a murderer right after you were shot? Are you kidding me right now? They haven't even found the guy who did this to you. He could still be trying to kill you. I've been so worried about you, and now you tell me you were gone, and... and my mom knew this and didn't tell me? And I even spoke to you during that time, on the phone, and... so... you lied to me and said you were still at my mom's place? Who are you, Eva Rae? I don't even recognize you anymore."

With that, he turned on his heel and walked into the bedroom, slamming the door shut behind him. I sat down on the couch, feeling lousy. I knew I had screwed up. I should never have lied to him. I felt tears in my eyes but wiped them away when Christine called from the kids' bedroom. There was no time to feel sorry for myself. Not now.

As I came into the room, the girls were fighting over a toy, a stupid doll that was so ugly I didn't understand why either of them wanted it. I watched them scream at one another for a few seconds, then closed the door, wondering when it would be my turn to scream.

I didn't get to finish the thought before my phone vibrated on the table, and I went for it.

# Chapter 65

"Thanks for coming all the way out here."

Mindy sat down on the bed of the motel room. She hid her hands behind her back so he wouldn't notice how much they were shaking. Stefan Mark stared at her for a few seconds, then sat down on the other bed. She noticed he had a gun in his back pocket. She couldn't blame him for being careful.

"I had to see what you wanted. But make it fast. I have someone waiting for me."

She swallowed. Her heart felt heavy. "Well, I guess we're both running now. I saw that you shot that FBI agent."

Stefan didn't reply. She hadn't expected him to.

"Let's cut the small talk. What do you want?" he asked.

"I-I need money. To go underground. Or else I might... you know... accidentally speak to the police and tell them everything."

He exhaled. "I had a feeling that's where we were heading."

Mindy nodded while biting her nails. It was hard for her to sit still. "I have to leave. I have to get out of here as fast as possible. My cousin is dead. Tuck is... dead. They're coming for me."

"How much do you need?"

She rubbed her nose. "About five hundred thousand should do. Enough to get me to the west coast and buy a condo somewhere, maybe. Start a new life."

"I feel like we've had this conversation before," Stefan said. "And yet you never left, you and Tuck."

"Well, we couldn't at that moment. He had a sick mother, and then we split up, as you remember. But we kept our word to you, and we never told anyone the truth about what happened to Arlene."

Stefan rose to his feet and hovered above Mindy.

"Don't you dare say her name!"

She lifted her hands resignedly. She was trying not to show him how scared she actually was.

"I'm sorry. I'm sorry. I won't do it again. Geez."

Stefan sat back down, nostrils still flaring. He was obviously fighting to keep calm.

"So… can I get the money?" she asked. "I need to know now."

Stefan bit the side of his cheek, then nodded.

"Yeah, I'll make sure you get it. But this is the last of it; you hear me? You give me the evidence."

Mindy shook her head nervously. "I might need more money at some point, and you never know what might happen."

Stefan pulled out his gun and placed it on her cheek, a pulsating vein popping out on his forehead.

"I wouldn't do that if I were you," she said, her voice sounding determined even though it was trembling. "I still have the evidence and hid it well, but if anything happens to me, the police get it."

It was a lie. It was in the safe in the motel room they were sitting in. She didn't know how to make sure the police got it if she died, but it sounded good—almost like a movie. And he bought it. The gun came down, and he put it back in his pants.

It was almost too easy.

"I'll get the money to you, but then no more, you hear me?" he said, walking to the door. He turned around as he opened it. "You give me the evidence, and it's over. I never want to hear from you again; do you understand? I don't even want to hear someone say your name."

"Make sure it's cash," she said as he slammed the door shut behind him. Mindy breathed, relieved, then fell back onto the bed with a deep sigh, surprised at her own courage.

# Chapter 66

"He's an assassin. I thought you better hear it from me."

It was my supervisor, Isabella Horne, who had called. She was talking about Stefan Mark, the guy that had shot me. They still hadn't found him, but the search was on in the entire country for the man who shot an FBI agent.

"Really?"

"Yes, he is originally from Bosnia, and during the Yugoslavian war, he worked as a mercenary. He ran away and came to the U.S. in 2000, where he also changed his name. His real name is Stefan Marković."

I sat down in a chair behind me. "I'll be…."

"Sounds like he knows how to kill," Isabella continued.

"You're thinking he might be the one who killed Arlene?"

"You tell me; you're the profiler, but you were looking for someone who was a skilled killer, right? That's what you said to me in this office when you persuaded me to give you the case. I think you were on the track of something big here when you approached him, and he shot you. I mean, you only shoot at an officer if you feel guilty about something, right? It's textbook."

I hung up, thinking about Alice Romano, Andrew Elrod, and

198

Tuck Bowman. They had all been killed in the same MO, a single stab to the heart. Death had occurred within thirty seconds, the medical examiner had concluded. It was precise, silent, and somewhat merciful since death would happen so fast; there would be barely any suffering.

Could it be Stefan Mark?

It seemed possible, and the thought kept brewing inside me, fueling new anger toward him. He was their neighbor across the street. He probably lied about seeing Frank Woods that morning, just like we knew that Alice Romano had.

But why?

I mean, I understood why he lied to cover his own tracks, but why did Alice? And how did Tuck and Mindy play into this? Mindy had made the call to nine-one-one. And now, she was on the run, her cousin and ex-boyfriend both dead. It had to be Stefan who was tracking them down, right?

Because they knew he was the one who killed Arlene. They were probably both there and saw him.

I nodded and smiled secretively. Yes, it fit well together. I still didn't know why Stefan wanted Arlene dead, but maybe....

I rose to my feet as the thought hit me.

*She had a lover.*

Arlene had a lover, and that's why she and Frank were getting a divorce. That was all in the files. No one ever found out who that lover was. The investigators weren't very interested in him since several witnesses soon came forward and said they had seen Frank. But it was in the books, the ones I found among Arlene's things. The person had said that she had to be "careful with the man she was seeing." You wouldn't say that about someone's husband. But definitely about a lover. So someone knew Stefan was dangerous, but who?

Who had written in those books and sent them to Arlene to warn her?

# Chapter 67

**T**HEN:
 She was led into an interrogation room. She had never been inside of a police station before, and everything about this scared her half to death. Mary Ellen's heart was pounding in her chest as she sat down. The two men who had introduced themselves as Detectives Price and Peterson sat across the table from her. They were both big, sturdy guys. Peterson was bald, while the other, Price, still had a decent head of hair. Peterson seemed to be the oldest and the one in charge. Price was young, probably early thirties, she guessed, whereas Peterson was at least fifty, maybe even more. Both had stern faces that terrified Mary Ellen.

"H-have I done something wrong?" she asked, looking from one to the other, feeling confused. They hadn't wanted to say anything in the car while driving to the station, and it made her even more nervous. Was she being accused of something? Did it have anything to do with her children?

Was she in trouble?

Detective Peterson cleared his throat. Mary Ellen wondered for a quick second if he had grown the mustache to compensate for the lack of hair on his head. It was a weird thing to think about in this situation, she told herself.

"Mary Ellen Garton?"

Her eyes met his, and she felt a pinch in her stomach. "Y-yes?"

Peterson sighed. He pulled out a photo and pushed it across the table for her to see.

"Th-that's Ethan?"

Peterson nodded slowly. "Do you recognize him?"

"Yes, of course. He's my boyfriend, and we live together. Is that what this is about? Him? Does it have to do with his visa? Is he here illegally?"

Peterson shook his head. "That is not why we're here, no."

She looked down at the picture in confusion, then up at Peterson. "Then, what is it? Has he done something?"

"You say you live together, but are you aware that he is also living with another woman and her children?"

Mary Ellen stared at them. She shook her head. "N-no. Ethan? No. My Ethan? No... no, you must have the wrong guy. Not Ethan, no."

She looked at Peterson, expecting him to agree with her, for him to tell her it was a joke or that, of course, it was the wrong guy. But he didn't move; his face remained cold as stone.

"I mean, he's not perfect, but..."

They still didn't react, while Mary Ellen felt panic rush through every fiber of her body. They had to believe her. They had to understand that they were wrong. She knew her Ethan.

"He would never do that."

"We understand, ma'am," Peterson said, then slid another picture across the table toward her.

"We understand that it might be a hard pill to swallow," Price said. "But we have photos."

"Here are photos of him and his family, his other family," Peterson said and put a finger on the photo.

Mary Ellen felt her lip quivering while she grabbed the photo and lifted it to see it better. In the picture, she saw Ethan holding hands with another woman while carrying a child, a little girl, on his shoulders.

She lowered the photo and put it back on the table, fighting her tears. "O-okay," she said, biting back sobs. "What do you want me to do about it? It's hardly illegal, even though it is a terrible thing to do. We're not married."

Peterson sighed again. His sighs had become very unpleasant to Mary Ellen.

"That's not all," he said. "There's more."

# Chapter 68

"Did Arlene have an affair with your neighbor, Stefan Mark?"

Frank Woods stared at me from the doorway. It was early in the morning, and he looked like he had just woken up.

"Well, good morning to you too," he said. "What do you want?"

"I need you to start talking, Frank. Because I am trying to keep you out of jail here, and you're not exactly making it easy for me. I do believe that Stefan murdered Arlene; I just don't know why. Can I come in?"

I didn't wait for his answer but walked straight past him. He shut the door behind me. I studied him. I didn't understand why it was so hard for me to figure him out.

I placed my hands on my hips. "Could Stefan have taken the children?"

"Why would he?"

"That's what I don't know," I said with an exhale. "I was hoping that maybe you knew."

He tilted his head. "If I knew, then I'd tell you; believe me. I need those kids back."

I blinked. There it was again—that strange phrase. He *needed* them.

"Why?" I asked, then waited for his reaction.

"What do you mean *why*?"

"You're their stepfather, right? You got custody after Arlene died because their father was dead, and you had been in their lives since they were very young, while their aunt lived out of state and had no relations with them at the time. Arlene had appointed you as designated caretaker in case of her death."

"Yes, and?"

I shook my head. "Nothing."

He scrutinized me. "I don't like your questions. Is there any particular reason you're here?"

"You never answered my first question. You said in your initial statement that you knew Arlene had a lover. Was that Stefan Mark? The guy who lived across the street?"

Frank sighed and rubbed his forehead. "Yes. Okay? You happy?"

"Why didn't you tell anyone back then?" I asked. "Why didn't you say so when the kids went missing?"

He hid his face in his hands. "I don't know, okay?"

"I don't believe that. Stefan testified against you and said he saw you come home early that morning when Arlene died. Why didn't you tell anyone that he had a motive for wanting you out of the way? I don't get it?"

He didn't say anything, so I continued, "Why did you say you killed your wife?"

"Because I don't remember, okay?" He looked at me, his eyes blood red, both his fists clenched. "I was drunk that night, and I have no clue what I was doing. I got drunk and then fought with Arlene. Then she left, and I never saw her again. When they said that witnesses had seen me, I believed them. I didn't know whether it was true or not. I mean, I didn't think I could, but I was so mad. I was so angry with her for sleeping with that guy. I just… I lost it, and yes, to be honest, I believed I had done it. I wanted to. I wanted to hurt her for what she had done to me. Besides, if I had told the police about Stefan, I was certain no one would believe me. I had reason to want to discredit him since he was a witness against me, and he was sleeping with my wife. I had no proof to back up my accusations. Stefan had another witness who backed up his statement."

"But this wasn't a jealousy murder," I said and placed a hand on his shoulder. "This was a premeditated murder done by a highly skilled killer like Stefan Mark."

Frank nodded and wiped his eyes. "But only you could see it. Thank you so much for not giving up on this. I can't thank you enough."

"Well, thank me when we get the children back," I said. "That's what matters right now. I need you to tell me everything you know about Stefan Mark."

# Chapter 69

The small cabin he had rented was cold at night, and Stefan put more wood in the fireplace to warm it up before bedtime. He sat on Ben's bed and started reading the book they had chosen. Luckily, the cabin came with lots of books and games, so the children managed to keep busy during the day. There was also a tire swing outside in the big tree and lots of yard to play in, so they didn't get too bored.

Izzy came in and crawled up in the bed with them, and Stefan had just begun to read the first page when she stopped him.

"How long are we supposed to stay here?"

Both kids looked up at him with big eyes, and his heart sank. There had been a lot of changes in their lives this year, and he couldn't blame them for being confused. Heck, their entire lives had been one big mess, especially since losing their mother six years ago.

It made him sad for them.

"I don't know," he said. "We need to be patient. But as I told you, it is important that we hide."

"But why are we running from Frank?" Izzy asked.

"Yeah, I like Frank," Ben chimed in. "He's always been nice."

Stefan nodded. "I know, kids. I know. But you have to trust me on this, okay?"

"And where is Aunt Pat?" Izzy asked. "You said she'd be here."

"I miss her," Ben said.

"She was our mother for like six years; you do realize that, right?" Izzy said, sounding suddenly very adult for a ten-year-old.

"And I've told her to meet us here," Stefan said, then wished he could just go back to reading the book. It was a lie, of course. He hadn't told anyone he had taken the kids, nor where they were hiding. He couldn't risk it. The kids were used to him since he would come in their house often and take care of stuff while Frank was out of town, sometimes for an entire month at a time. That's when he fell in love with Arlene, and everything changed.

"I miss Mommy," Izzy said and lowered her eyes. "I can barely remember her anymore, and that makes me sad."

"Can I see her picture again on your phone?" Ben asked.

Stefan found his phone and the pictures he had of Arlene, then let the kids scroll through them. It was an old phone that wasn't in his name, so the police couldn't trace it. The one they thought was his, he had left at the house.

"I miss her too, kids. Believe me. Every day."

Izzy looked up at him. "So, who killed her? If it wasn't Frank?"

Stefan smiled softly. "That's a very good question. It's getting late. How about we get back to reading, so you two can get a good night's sleep?"

"I miss my bike," Ben said.

"I'll run into town and look for a new one tomorrow; how about that, huh?"

"Can I get one too?" Izzy asked, her eyes shining in the bright light from the lamp next to her. She looked so much like her mother that it almost hurt.

"Of course!" he said. "Heck, I might get one as well, and then we all can go biking in the trails outside the cabin. How about that, huh?"

"Yay," they both said in unison while Stefan sighed happily. If only they could remain like this forever.

# Chapter 70

It was late when I returned, and Chad didn't even say hello. He just looked up from his screen long enough to shake his head before grabbing his laptop and walking into the bedroom, where he shut the door behind him. The kids were already sleeping, and I peeked into their room just to get a glimpse of them. Chad hadn't spoken to me since the day I told him about Kentucky. Seeing him this way hurt, but I didn't really know what to do about it. So instead, I worked even harder and stayed away from home, just to avoid his sour looks. I had come back to the office and told Horne that I was ready to work again since I had no pain anymore, which she believed even though it was a big fat lie. I popped painkillers like candy and continued digging into this case, even though I was no longer assigned to it.

I didn't care anymore.

I pulled out my notes that I had written down on what Frank Woods told me about Stefan Mark. He didn't know much about him, so I had gone to his house afterward and ducked under the police tape, then walked inside to take a good look. A lot had been taken to the lab, but it hadn't brought them any closer to where he could be hiding with the children.

But there was one question that kept bothering me in all this.

Why? Why would he take Arlene's children?

It was one thing that he murdered Arlene and pinned it all on Frank so he could get away with it, but why take the children?

It made no sense.

Unless he just had it in for Frank so bad that he wanted to harm him and the children. But they weren't even Frank's children. He was just the stepdad. He had been in their lives since Arlene was pregnant with Ben when her husband died in a car accident. According to Frank, Stefan moved into the house across the street six months later, and they began their affair around a month after that. Frank traveled a lot and was often gone for weeks at a time, and that was when the affair started as far as he knew.

So why did Stefan kill Arlene?

I looked at my notes, then found my phone where I had taken photos inside Stefan Mark's house. I scrolled through them, stopping now and then and zooming into one to see if there could be something I had missed.

"Where are you hiding?"

Could he have taken them back to Bosnia?

I shook my head. No, he was already a wanted man after shooting me, and he would be stopped in the airport.

I looked at my arm and touched it, then winced in pain. I found the pain killers, then popped a few and washed them down with water, hoping they'd act fast. I thought about the day in his yard when he had pulled the trigger at me, then paused.

If Stefan was such a skilled killer, why didn't he kill me? Why was I still alive? He shot me at close range, so it had to have been deliberate. He had only have wanted to stop me, not kill me.

Right?

*You have no idea what you have done.*

That's what he said to me right before he fired the gun. What did he mean by that?

I returned to the photos, scrolling through them when something caught my eye. Something I should have seen earlier, but for some reason, didn't.

I shut off my phone, grabbed my car keys, and hurried for the door. I wondered for a second if I should tell Chad where I was going but realized he probably didn't care, then left without a word to him.

# Chapter 71

THEN:

"We have been keeping an eye on your boyfriend for quite some time," Peterson continued. Price had left and come back, bringing them all waters, and Mary Ellen sipped her plastic bottle, feeling like the floor had opened beneath her and was about to suck her down into the dark abyss. She tried to focus on Peterson's mole close to his lower lip that kept moving as he talked. She felt like if she kept her focus on that small dot moving, she could remain calm and not break down. It was all she could do right now.

Peterson cleared his throat, then pushed another picture toward her. "Do you recognize this man?"

Mary Ellen took her eyes off the mole and looked down at the photo.

"Do you know him?" Price asked.

Mary Ellen nodded. "That's Ethan's friend, Peter. He stops by sometimes, and they have a beer while sitting in the garage. They know each other from some school they went to, I think."

Peterson nodded, then took the picture back and placed it inside the yellow folder. "Okay."

"H-he's only been over a few times. I don't think they're very close."

"Has he ever been over when Ethan wasn't home?" Price asked, folding his hands on the table in front of him.

"Well… yes, he came over once when Ethan was overseas. I invited him to stay for dinner."

The two detectives exchanged a glance. It made Mary Ellen uncomfortable. "What's going on here? What are you trying to tell me?"

She looked at her watch. It was late afternoon now, and the kids had come home from school. They would start to ask where their mother was. She had texted Ethan and told him she was stuck in traffic downtown and wouldn't be home until late. It was a terrible lie, but she couldn't come up with anything better, and she didn't want him to know where she really was.

Peterson took the word. He looked into her eyes, then said, "We believe this man has come to take your children."

Mary Ellen stared at him. She realized she wasn't breathing.

"What?"

Price nodded. "We suspect they both work for the same trafficking ring. The plan is to take your children and send them overseas where they'll be sold into… well, prostitution most likely."

"Both? What do you mean both?" she asked, her voice getting high and pitchy. "Who?"

"Your boyfriend and his friend," Price said. "We don't know their real names since they operate under different identities everywhere they go."

"It's their MO to find single mothers," Peterson said. "And one of them gets close to her and acts as her boyfriend for months, maybe even years, and then they kidnap the children and take them overseas with them. To Europe. They meet the women online in dating apps. They start by love-bombing their victims, you know— smothering them with sweet words and gifts, telling them they love them early on, sending flowers and chocolate, all the stuff. They basically make it impossible for the women to say no, and then when she is in the net, they start to push her boundaries. They ask for money to help with a business adventure or a lawyer's fee or something, and then when that works, they know they can keep pushing and make sure the woman doesn't suspect a thing, that she is—sorry for my bluntness—naive enough to believe anything they tell her. They might even start beating up their victims and abuse them mentally to keep them from believing their own judgment—gaslighting them, breaking them. Sometimes, they'll marry the woman to make things smoother, but not always. They get close with the kids, so it's easier to take them once it comes to that. They'll go willingly because they know them. No one will suspect a thing onboard the plane since the men are close with the children and interact like a family. We've seen cases where they got the mom to sign a consent form by saying it's required, but that form actually permits them to take the children onboard a plane even if they don't share a last name. They persuade them to get the children passports, telling her they want to take the entire family to visit their hometown and family over there. But then they leave without the mom. One day, she comes home, and they're all just gone."

Price found another folder and opened it. "This is another mother who lost her three children two years ago. And this one is another case where both the two children and the mother disappeared out of the blue. They were last seen traveling to Greece. We're working with Interpol and have traced one of her children to some brothel in Athens where she was rescued. But as soon as they leave the country, it becomes almost impossible to follow their tracks."

"That's why we wanted to get you in here and warn you," Peterson said. "So far, we haven't been able to prove any of this, so we can't touch either of the men yet. They keep changing names and coming into the country with new identities. They avoid pictures being taken with the women they're with, stating they don't like social media or having their pictures taken. They're very clever and have been doing this for God knows how long. But we're keeping a close eye on them, and at some point, they will make a mistake."

"That's where we hoped you might come in," Price took over.

Mary Ellen stared from one to the other. "You want me to spy for you?"

"Well, not exactly; just keep a close eye on these two men and maybe take some pictures of them with the children without them seeing it, and maybe let us know if they do anything that we could get them in for. It doesn't have to have to do with the trafficking; it could be something else they did—a traffic violation or even just beating you up."

She narrowed her eyes. Panic was erupting rapidly through her body. She couldn't believe any of what she was hearing.

"Do you know what you've done?" she asked and rose abruptly to her feet, pushing the chair back across the floor. "Do you even realize what you have done by bringing me down here today?"

They looked at her.

"You've made sure that my kids were left alone with him. They've been alone for three hours now. I signed that darn consent form because he said I had to. I got them passports so we could all visit his half-brother and mother in Poland, with whom he had just reconciled and finally gotten his business back. But I guess that was all just another lie, huh? It was all just a lie?"

Mary Ellen could barely breathe, and her chest felt so tight and constricted. She grabbed her purse and rushed toward the door, screaming at the top of her lungs, "Three hours. For crying out loud. Three hours."

## Chapter 72

In the darkness, the house looked even creepier than it had earlier when I had been inside. I ducked under the tape, then went up to the porch and through the front door. I walked inside the living room, then found the paper bin by the desk in Stefan Mark's office.

I saw it in the picture I had taken earlier, but now I was staring at it in real life. I had put on plastic gloves so I wouldn't mess up anything, then reached down and grabbed the book from the full paper bin. It was a copy of a book called *A Walk in the Woods* by Bill Bryson. I didn't know it, but I had seen it before.

Among Arlene's things.

I opened it to the first page and looked at the inscription.

*You won't get away with it.*

I stared at the words and recognized the handwriting from the books I had found in Arlene's boxes. I had brought one of them, and I held it up next to this one to be sure. There was no doubt. It was the same person who had tried to warn Arlene about the man she was seeing. Her lover.

Stefan Mark.

But who was this person giving them these books? And why?

I sat down in a chair, staring at the book's cover when my phone rang, and I picked it up.

"Rachel from research here."

"Well, hi there, Rachel from research. What's up?"

"You told me to look into that woman? The one with the children? You were wondering where they were?"

"That's right. There were toys, but they seemed to have been left unused for years, and the beds too. It seemed odd to me. Her name was Mary Ellen something."

"Garton."

"That's her, yes."

"I can't find anything," Rachel said.

"What?"

"The father left her alone with four children. He lives upstate but hasn't seen the children since he left nine years ago. I called him earlier to check."

"And they can't have been taken to foster care or something?"

"They're not in the system. They were signed up to the local elementary school, but they said they haven't seen them in six years. They just didn't show up anymore, and the school assumed they had moved out of state, but the mother simply forgot to tell them. It happens, they said."

I leaned back in the recliner, rubbing my forehead. "What the... Is there at least a missing person's report?"

"Nope. I ran a search in all the missing person's archives in the state and didn't find anything."

"That's very odd," I said.

"I'll keep looking, but I thought you should know."

"Thanks."

I hung up and stared at the book in my hand, turning it in the light from the lamp next to me. There was still so much I didn't understand, but a picture was beginning to take shape in my mind.

And I didn't like it at all.

I looked at the book description on the back of the book, then read it. It seemed to be a hiker's guide to the Appalachian Trail. I kept staring at the words on the back, biting my cheek, wondering why Stefan Mark had thrown this book out right before he left.

Could I be so lucky?

It was worth a try.

# Part VI

TWO DAYS LATER

## Chapter 73

It was freezing outside as fall was coming to an end and winter was knocking. Stefan didn't have enough warm clothes for the children, so he put that on the list of things to buy once they made it to the town. It was just a small mountain town, but it had what they needed. And he had promised them those bikes, even though it would soon be too cold to ride them.

"Can I get a blue one?" Ben asked, his eyes gleaming with excitement. "I always wanted a blue bike."

"I just want a purple one. Anything but pink; it's so childish," Izzy said.

"Yes. You can both have any color you want," Stefan said absentmindedly. He glared at the bag in the seat next to him, containing all the money.

Five hundred thousand. Cash.

He had told her to meet him by the hardware store, and as he drove into the parking lot, he spotted her sitting in her car. He parked, then turned to look at the kids in the back seat.

"Why are we stopping here?" Ben asked.

"I just gotta do something first. Then we'll go get the bikes, okay?"

Ben looked disappointed. "Aw."

"It will only take a few minutes, okay?"

Izzy looked at her brother. "It's okay. We can wait."

Stefan smiled, then ruffled her hair. He grabbed the bag, opened the door, and stepped out.

"Be right back. Stay put."

Stefan slammed the door shut and looked around him, scanning the area to ensure no one was watching him. There were a lot of cars in the parking lot, but no people other than an elderly woman walking past him, pushing her cart filled with plants she had just bought. Stefan hurried to the car and got into the passenger seat.

Mindy's eyes lingered on him. It was obvious she was nervous. Her eyes gave her away. "Is it all there?"

He handed her the sports bag. "You see for yourself."

She unzipped it and looked inside, then nodded. "Looks good."

"But that means it ends here," he said.

She nodded. "Okay. I'll be out of your hair. I'll leave right away, and you won't see me again."

"That's not enough. I want the evidence."

She nodded. "All right."

Mindy reached into her pocket, then pulled out an old Samsung flip phone and handed it to him. Stefan smiled.

"I hope I never have to see your face again."

He grabbed the door handle and pulled it, then stepped outside. He didn't see the person waiting for him outside until too late, and a gun was placed in front of his eyes, and he slowly sat back down inside.

Hands reached down and searched for his gun, then found it in his belt and pulled it out. A red-haired woman stuck her head close to his.

"We don't want any more accidents, do we? I'm still recovering from our last meet and greet."

# Chapter 74

**T**HEN:

 "Sam? Sammy?"

Mary Ellen pushed open the front door. It was left ajar, which made her heart stop. She called her firstborn's name again and again, but when no answer came, she continued to the other children.

"Jennifer? Lucas?"

She was met by nothing but a wall of silence from inside her own house. Fear tore through her body, ripping open her heart.

"Millie? Oh, dear God, Millie, please."

Even thinking about her youngest made her clasp her chest in pain. Where was she? Where were all of them? In the yard?

She ran to the back, but it was empty, then continued up the stairs, running through each and every bedroom, screaming their names at the top of her lungs.

Still nothing but silence.

"Sammy?" she tried from the top again, running into her own bedroom, checking every corner like she expected them to be hiding from her, and this was all just a game. She rushed down the stairs as she heard a noise, but then realized it was the detectives, who had brought her home in their police car. Peterson and Price walked inside, and Mary Ellen ran down the stairs, screaming, "They're not here. They're not HERE. Where are they? Tell me where they are? WHERE?"

She ran toward Peterson, her fists clenched, then started to hammer on his chest, crying and screaming.

"It's all your fault. You did this. You did this!"

"Ma'am, you need to calm down, please."

He held her wrists, and she stopped hitting, then fell to her knees, sobbing.

"They're gone. They're gone."

Breathing raggedly, bending forward, tears running down her cheeks, her stomach in pain, her torso shaking, she sobbed and cried.

"They took them. They took my children!"

"Ma'am," Peterson said and placed a hand on her back. "You need to...."

She looked up, and their eyes met. Peterson stepped back, surprised at the massive amount of grief and anger in her eyes. Mary Ellen rose to her feet, then approached him.

"You go find them. You know who took them. Go arrest them."

He put a hand on his gun. "Ma'am, I need you to step back...."

"You're not even sorry, are you? You're not even sorry that you dragged me down to the police station and let me leave my children alone with a dangerous kidnapper who wants to... sell them into prostitution? You're not sorry you tried to warn me while he was running away with them? Can't you see it? Can't you see that you did this? It's all your fault. If I hadn't been down at the station with you, talking, then I would have been here to protect my children."

"Ma'am, we need you to back up...." Price said and held out one hand while the other went for his weapon.

Mary Ellen stared at them, unable to fully grasp the situation.

"Well, do something!" she yelled. "Don't just stand there!"

"We are doing everything we can, ma'am, but you need to calm down now!" Price yelled, pulling his gun.

"Calm down? You want me to calm down? How am I supposed

to do that when my kids were taken, and you're just standing around? Why aren't you doing anything? Do something!"

Mary Ellen screamed at the top of her lungs, then lifted a fist and slammed it into Peterson's chest once again. Next thing, she was on the floor, a knee in her neck and both of them yelling at her.

## Chapter 75

"I need you to get out of the car. Both of you."

I held the gun tightly between my hands. I wasn't taking any chances with this guy this time. He held his hands in the air, then stepped out. I had the local police with me, and their officers had surrounded the area, blocking the entrance to the parking lot with their cruisers.

Stefan Mark looked down at me, and I could tell he knew he was defeated. I stared at Mindy Lynn across the roof of the car while an officer searched her and took the sports bag from inside the vehicle.

The local officers booked them, and we all went back to their small station, where I got to interview them separately. They only had one interrogation office, so I started with Stefan Mark. I grabbed the sports bag and placed it on the table in front of him.

"That's the money," I said and looked at Stefan. "For Mindy to keep quiet and not tell what she really saw that night that Arlene died. Right? To keep Frank in jail because you needed him in there. That's why you paid her off back then, and that's why you're doing it again." I pulled out the flip phone and placed it on the table. "And the pictures are all on this, right? This is the evidence she used to blackmail you. She took pictures of whoever killed Arlene six years ago, and all I need is to get this charged somehow, and then I can see for myself, am I right?"

Stefan nodded. "She was the one who came to me back then—her and her boyfriend, Tuck. They wanted money to keep quiet. They said they had pictures. So, I paid them. But they blackmailed me because they knew I had said something else in my testimony. They knew I had lied and thought they could get some more money out of me, which they could."

"You told the police you saw Frank Woods come home that morning, and you even paid off Alice Romano to back up your story. All this because you wanted Frank Woods in jail?" I asked. "And he was so drunk that night, and fighting with Arlene when she left, so he wouldn't be able to say what he really did; he didn't have an alibi."

Stefan nodded. "Yes. He belongs in jail. I was only in all this because I owed money to Frank. I never wanted to do those things we did."

"Those things. You mean trafficking kids overseas? Frank was going to take Arlene's kids? Is that why you kidnapped them? So he couldn't take them to Bosnia with him? I saw the tickets on his counter in the house. He was planning on taking the kids with him now that he was their sole guardian. Was he going to sell them?"

Stefan gave me a serious look. "Yes."

"You did all this to protect the children? You knew that when Arlene died, he'd get custody, and then he could do whatever he wanted. He could take them overseas, and then who knew where they'd end up?"

He nodded. "I told Patricia, Arlene's sister, and we decided to make up a story, making sure Frank became the suspect."

"So, you lied?"

He nodded again.

"So, we lied."

"But it was okay because it was for a good cause," I said. "Right?"

"Yes. It was to save the children from a fate in trafficking. You have no idea what they do to those kids. I couldn't let it happen."

"And you got away with it for six whole years."

"Until you came along and ruined everything," he said. "You reopened the case, and suddenly he was out. He got the children and was about to take them away when I realized I had to stop him."

"You took them away."

He exhaled. "Yes. I took them to safety."

"But you were stupid enough to rent the cabin in the mountains in Arlene's name. That was probably not very well planned. It made it pretty easy for us to track you down once I found the book in your home and knew where to look. Then we bugged the landline belonging to the cabin, and that's how we knew you were meeting with Mindy to give her the money and get the pictures."

He sighed. I pushed the book toward him.

"I also saw the inscription," I said. "Someone was onto you. The same someone that also warned Arlene, right?"

He became quiet. He was fiddling with the book between his fingers. I leaned back in the chair.

"You fell in love, didn't you? With Arlene?"

He stared at me, barely blinking.

"It wasn't supposed to happen," I continued. "You were supposed to be the good neighbor. That was your role in yours and Frank's little act. Like it was with all the other women you had tricked over the years, whose children you stole. You were to play the good Samaritan who came over to help when Frank wasn't home, making them all trust you, and then, together with Frank, you were supposed to take the children out of the country. But you fell for her, didn't you? You got too involved, and suddenly you couldn't do it. You couldn't take the children from the woman you loved so dearly. Am I right?"

A tear escaped the corner of his eyes, but he wiped it away quickly. "Is it important anymore? I'm done no matter what I say, right?"

"Maybe. The kids are being taken to their aunt now, and Frank

Woods is also being taken in. But if you help us by telling the truth, I'm sure the FBI will make a deal with you and maybe lower your sentence. We want the names of everyone who is involved both here and overseas. We want all of them."

"O-okay."

"And then I need you to tell me who really killed Arlene."

Stefan Mark scoffed. "That's the thing."

"What do you mean?"

He threw out both his hands.

"The thing is, I don't know who killed her."

"You're telling me you've never seen the pictures that Mindy and Tuck took that night?" I asked.

"No."

I grabbed the phone in my hand and looked at it. "I guess we'll have to find a charger, then. Where the heck do I find a charger for a Samsung?"

## Chapter 76

L ainie Gable yawned. She closed her eyes for a few seconds while the two children continued their play. They were the last two left for the day; all the other children had been picked up long ago.

Why was it always those two?

Some parents were just so irresponsible. It was almost six o'clock, and Lainie was the last adult there. She really needed to be able to leave at six like she was supposed to. The preschool closed at six o'clock. Didn't these parents know?

Or did they simply not care?

Lainie exhaled and thought about her boyfriend. They had been in a fight the night before, as usual, and she had barely slept. Today, he had been texting her all day, being passive-aggressive, and it was exhausting. She had promised to stop by to see her mom, who sat alone in her condo and could barely move after her hip surgery. Lainie and her sister took turns bringing her dinner and eating with her so that she wouldn't be alone. But to be honest, Lainie would give anything she had to be able just to go home and lie on the couch or even go to bed early.

Gosh, she hated being hungover at work. It was the worst.

Lainie closed her eyes again and a pain shot through her head. She'd had this splitting headache all day. Why had she drunk so much wine the night before? She knew it always ended badly. But George had been acting out, telling her how terrible a mother she was to their son, and she just couldn't take it anymore. So, yes, she popped open a bottle of white wine and started to drink to calm herself. To shut out his voice in her head, telling her she wasn't good enough. But that only gave him more ammunition. Now, he could yell at her for drinking as well, calling her a drunk.

At least she waited until the kid was in bed. And it wasn't like she did it every night. She usually only drank on the weekends. But last night, she just couldn't cope with it anymore.

*When are these darn parents going to come and pick up their children?*

Lainie looked at the two sisters. They were playing in the toy kitchen, the four-year-old baking something that the two-year-old tasted. But now, the two-year-old didn't want to play that game anymore, and she cast her love on some toy animals, especially the giraffe that she put in her mouth. When her sister realized she had lost her attention, she tried to force her to taste her imaginary food, but the little one refused. Seconds later, the big one was yelling at the little one, the little one crying loudly. Lainie sighed and went to grab the youngest in her arms, taking her away from her older sister.

"Olivia, if Christine doesn't want to play your game anymore, then leave her alone, okay?"

A noise by the door made Lainie turn around, and as a woman poked her head inside, she smiled, relieved.

"You're here to pick up Christine and Olivia?"

The woman nodded. "Yes."

Lainie walked toward her and handed her Christine, happy to get the kid out of her arms. She was so tired she could cry right now. But as she gave her the child, she realized she hadn't seen this woman before and paused.

"Say, are you on the pick-up list?" she asked. "I don't believe I've seen you here before."

"I'm on the list, yes," she said.

"Okay, can I see some ID, please?" Lainie asked.

The woman handed her a driver's license, and Lainie looked at it. The list was in the office in the main building that she had already locked up, hoping to leave quickly. In order to check if this woman was actually on the list, she'd have to go all the way up there and unlock everything. She really didn't have the energy for that, and it would make her even later. The woman smiled and looked at her, seeming sincere enough.

"I'm a friend of the family," the woman said. "They both were held up at work today. The dad is out of town."

Lainie nodded. Yes, usually, the kids were only picked up late when the mother was supposed to pick them up. Often the grandmother would come, but she probably had better things to do today. Lainie liked the grandmother a lot.

*It's probably fine.*

Lainie handed her the driver's license back with a smile. "Their backpacks are by the door, packed and ready to go."

The woman grabbed the children's hands in hers.

"Come on. Let's get you home."

# Chapter 77

After spending two days in the mountains, I had promised Chad I'd pick up the girls on the way back since he had a meeting out of town and would be home late. But as I drove back, I got stuck in traffic, and when I arrived, it was only five minutes until six o'clock. We hadn't been able to find a charger for the Samsung phone at the small police station up there, so I had brought it with me back to our own IT guys who could probably get the pictures out of it somehow. I felt confident that I would soon have a very good picture of Arlene's killer. Stefan wasn't our guy; I had realized it after interrogating him for hours. He really did love her and was destroyed when she was killed.

So, who was?

I parked the car and got out, thinking I'd made it just in time, then ran for the door and pulled the handle.

It was locked.

"What the...?"

Remembering that they were usually open until six, I knocked.

Nothing.

I looked in the window, but it was dark inside the pre-school. I knocked again.

"Hello?"

Only silence.

*What's going on here?*

I knocked again, this time harder.

"Hello? I'm here to pick up my children? Hello? Christine? Olivia?"

When there was still no response, I began to get nervous. Had I missed something? Had Miranda maybe picked them up earlier? Had Chad called her because he didn't trust I'd make it? Or had Chad picked them up himself?

I found my cell phone and called him.

"Do you have the girls?"

"Excuse me?" he said.

"Do you have the kids?"

"Uhm, no. You were supposed to pick them up."

"I know," I said with a deep, frustrated exhale. "But they're not here. It's locked. The door is locked."

"What are you saying?" he asked, sounding anxious. "Who has them then?"

I scanned the area and suddenly saw a woman by a door further down that she was in the middle of locking. I told Chad I'd call him back and hung up. Then I ran after her as she was about to leave.

"Hi, hey, stop."

I caught up to her by her car.

"Sorry, we're closed," she said without looking up at me.

"I'm here to pick up my children," I said. "Christine and Olivia? Two and four years old?"

She lifted her gaze and gave me a strange look. "They were picked up just ten minutes ago."

"They were picked up? By who?" I asked, my voice shaking.

"Uh, this woman. Said she was a friend of the family."

"Was it their grandmother?"

"No, it wasn't her. It was someone else. Someone I hadn't met before."

"And you let her leave with them?" I almost yelled. How was this even possible? "You didn't check if she was on the pick-up list?

Because I don't have anyone else on that list except for me, their dad, and their grandmother. You should know that."

I could tell that the realization of what she had done was sinking in now. The woman stared at me, eyes growing wide, the corners of her mouth dropping.

"I… I thought… I mean, she…."

"Did you even get her name?" I asked.

"Yeah, yeah, I wrote it down; here, give me a sec," she said as she fumbled in her bag and took out the sign-out sheet. "I wrote it down just in case."

"Oh, well, just in case, huh?" I pulled the paper out of her hand and looked at the name.

I stared at the letters, while suddenly all the pieces fell into place, along with my world that fell apart.

"Oh, dear God."

# Chapter 78

I rushed through D.C. traffic, cursing loudly inside the car and panic erupting through my body. I couldn't stop thinking about Sydney, my sister who was stolen from the supermarket when I was only five years old and she was seven. I knew these things happened. Children were taken and never returned.

It was my worst nightmare.

"Oh, dear God, please, help me find them. Please, don't let her harm them."

I kept praying under my breath as I zigzagged through rush-hour traffic like a maniac, honking and yelling at the other cars, sometimes even going on the sidewalk to make it through.

*Why hadn't I seen it until now?*

I kept asking myself that question over and over again. It had been right under my nose all this time, right under my big fat nose.

And yet, I hadn't seen it.

As I reached the right street, I sped up, then stopped in front of the small house. A car was parked in the driveway, giving me hope that it was the right place. I had called for backup, and they would be here any minute now.

I just couldn't wait for them.

I rushed out of the car and up the porch. I knocked while panting loudly. "Hello? FBI. I'm coming in."

I kicked the door open while pulling out my gun from the holster, then held it in front of me.

"If you're in here, then lie down with your hands above your head. Any movement and I will shoot."

That was, of course, a lie since I wouldn't risk accidentally hurting either of my children. Of course not.

"Olivia? Christine?"

I could hear how bad my voice was trembling as I said their names. My heart was knocking against my rib cage, and I could barely breathe. I kept seeing my sister's eyes looking at me as the man dragged her away from me. I remember the sound of her calling my name just before she disappeared out the sliding doors. And then my mom's shaking voice, her hands as they grabbed me after realizing what happened. And then how they never touched me again because she couldn't deal with me anymore. Every time she looked at me, I reminded her of what had happened. For years, I dealt with her coldness and resentment toward me because he had taken Sydney and not me. Because I was still here and she was not. She blamed me. I knew she did. It was the only explanation I could ever come up with for her ice-cold nature toward me for the rest of my life growing up. Her pain could be felt through the entire house, every room she entered. I didn't want to end up like that. I didn't want to have to go through that same pain.

*Oh, dear Lord, please, let me have my children back.*

I heard the police cruisers come closer outside and stop, then heard the sound of a child's voice, and turned to look out the window.

A sigh of great relief rushed through my heart as I spotted Olivia on a swing in the backyard.

# Chapter 79

I hurried out the back door and stood on the porch. I spotted her sitting on the ground, a doll in her hand, looking at Christine standing in front of her. Seeing both my children made my heart gallop in my chest, and I walked quickly toward the playground in the back. I held the gun out in front of me, terrified of something accidentally happening to my children.

"Mary Ellen Garton," I said and walked closer. "You're under arrest...."

I didn't make it further before I stopped. I stared at my two-year-old daughter in front of me. Then my heart stopped.

Between her hands, she was holding a gun—a loaded gun.

Mary Ellen was watching her, tears rolling down her face. "I've missed them so much. I don't know where the other two are, though. Maybe they're inside?"

I froze, staring at the gun in my child's hands. Mary Ellen seemed to be in a different world. When I visited her the first time, I had sensed that something was completely off with her. I should have recognized the look in her eyes. After all, I had grown up seeing it in my mother's eyes.

Christine stared at the gun between her fingers, then turned it, and my heart skipped a beat. I was worried it would go off.

"Christine," I said. "Hand me that, please."

"Excuse me," Mary Ellen said, looking up at me, a sudden rush of anger going across her face. "Who are you? What are you doing here?"

"These are my children," I said, sweat springing to my face as I stared at the gun between my two-year-old's hands. I was afraid to make a sudden movement. Her finger was playing with the trigger, and if I scared her, she might accidentally pull it or drop it, and it might go off.

Mary Ellen rose to her feet. "No! These are my children. What are you doing here? Are you here to steal them? I can't let you steal my children."

Mary Ellen was crying heavily now, and I realized she had gotten lost somewhere in there—lost in her grief and sadness. She stared at the gun in my hand and looked terrified.

"Don't take my children; don't take them!"

I glared at her, then back down at Christine, who squealed and placed the tip of the barrel in her mouth.

"No, Christine, no!"

That's when Mary Ellen jumped me. I fell back into the grass, surprised by her sudden movement, and the gun was knocked out of my hand. Mary Ellen rained down punches on me, her eyes manic and mad.

"I won't let you take my children. I simply won't let you! I saw it in your eyes when you were here last time. You were checking out the bedrooms, looking for them. I followed you after you left and saw you with them. I knew you were the one who had taken them, and so I took them back."

She punched me on the nose, and I saw stars, then grabbed her wrist and bent it back until she screamed, then pushed her off me and rolled over until I was on top of her, panting.

She kicked me in the stomach, and I flew off. Then she went for my gun.

# Chapter 80

"Get out of my house!" Mary Ellen screamed as she hovered above me, pointing my own gun at me. I glared at Christine, who was still sucking on the tip of the gun, her fingers fiddling with the trigger, and I could barely breathe.

I heard the officers come up behind us, but I told them to back off, scared the children might get hurt.

"Please, Mary Ellen. These are my children. My daughters. You took them from me. I want them back. Do you remember what that's like? To lose your children? You wouldn't want that to happen to anyone, would you? To feel the pain you have. I know, Mary Ellen. I know what happened to you."

"You don't know anything about me," Mary Ellen said.

I sat up, holding out my hands to ensure she understood I wasn't trying to harm her. Out of the corner of my eye, I was keeping an eye on Christine and the gun.

"I know you were a Navy Seal. I saw the pictures of you in uniform in the hallway and the certificate of you being honored by the Navy Seals, and I had you checked out and read that you got hurt during deployment. You know how to kill. And you killed

240

Arlene. You sent her those books to warn her because you had lost your children."

"They were taken," she said, trailing off. "I thought I had found a man. The perfect man. But that's the thing, right? When it's too good to be true, it usually is. And we become blind. We see the little signs in the beginning. The lies, the inconsistencies. We ignore the small alarms that go off in our minds because it hurts too much and we want so badly to believe it isn't true. So we lie. To ourselves, to others. We tell them it's okay, we're okay. But we're not. And then all of a sudden it's too late."

Mary Ellen lowered the gun slightly. Our eyes met, and I saw the anger being replaced by profound sadness.

"It was a scam?" I asked.

She nodded and looked down briefly. "A trafficking ring, the police told me. But they couldn't prove it."

"So you saw that these men were allowed to continue. No one stopped them. You didn't want the same to happen to Arlene as well. You couldn't live with yourself if it did. And you certainly didn't trust the police to be able to help."

"She came to me; you know? She sent me a book back, saying she wanted to meet. And then her phone number. I called her up, and we met over lunch one day. I told her my story and showed her the few pictures I had of the guy who tricked me. As soon as she saw that it was the same guy, that it was Frank, her own husband, and I told her about the friend and described him to her, she knew it was bad. But then she wanted to go to the police, and I couldn't let her do that."

"Why not?"

"Because of what happened to me. I knew if she went to them, I would never see my children again. Only Ethan—or Frank as he called himself now—knew where they were. That's why I contacted him once he was released, and he came to my house. I needed him to tell me where my children were. I thought he would do that if I kept him out of jail—if I made sure all the evidence against him was removed, that all the liars were exposed. I told him that, and he got angry with me."

241

"Wait, what happened to you?"

"I was arrested. On the day my children went missing, the two detectives arrested me because I lost it. They roughed me up so badly that I had to go to the hospital. I was unconscious for weeks. And then, when their superior got the story, they were both fired. The case was archived. But that meant that Arlene was never warned. I saw her in the pictures that the detectives showed me with my Ethan and knew she was about to suffer the same fate as me. I couldn't let that happen. But I couldn't risk Frank realizing I was the one who warned her because then I might never see my children. So, I started to send her the books, warning her about them. But then she kept saying she'd go to the police, and that night when she... well, she and Frank had a terrible fight, and she left the house, then came to my house. She knocked on my door and told me we were going to the police. Together. In the middle of the night. I would tell them my story, and then she would tell them hers. Then they'd have to arrest him. I told her it wasn't enough and that she couldn't leave the kids alone with him. They were sleeping, she said, and Frank didn't know why she left. She needed to talk to the police. Right now. I got into the car with her and thought I could persuade her not to go—maybe by telling her what the police did to me. I didn't trust them at all. But she kept rambling on and on about it, and I had to... I had to stop her. I wanted to force Frank to take me to my children, but I knew if he ended up in the hands of the police, that would never happen. But she wouldn't listen."

"So, you stabbed her? In the car?"

Mary Ellen looked down at her hands, then nodded. "I did what I knew how to do, to make it quick and painless—right to the heart. And then we crashed. I didn't get hurt badly, so I jumped out of the car and grabbed the gas can from the back, then poured it on her body and set it on fire."

"You thought you'd get away with making it look like an accident," I said. "No one knew you were with her, so you could run away. But you forgot one thing. Someone saw you. Someone took your picture."

"I didn't see them and didn't realize it until much later."

"They kept quiet and decided to blackmail Stefan instead," I said. "Because at that point, he and Arlene's sister had already planned to get Frank sent down for the murder by lying. And as Mindy and Tuck realized this, they started to blackmail them. But you didn't want Frank in jail. You wanted him to stay out once he was released. So, you killed Alice Romano, Tuck, and tried to kill Mindy too. But she put up a fight, and you ended up killing her cousin instead while Mindy fled. Because they all knew the truth. Mindy hid in Kentucky, and Tuck was on his way to warn her when you got to him. Or maybe he even led you to her?"

Mary Ellen shook her head slowly and looked at her hands, tears running down her cheeks.

"I... I just wanted my children back. I needed Frank out of prison to get them. I have waited... six years without them. I don't even know what they look like anymore. They could pass me on the street, and I wouldn't even recognize them."

I stared at the woman in front of me, my heart breaking. I remembered thinking the very same thing about my sister—that if I saw her today, twenty-five years later, I wouldn't even recognize her.

A couple of tears escaped the corner of my eye as Mary Ellen dropped the gun in her hand and fell to her knees, crying. I rose to my feet and turned to look at Christine when I realized she was no longer holding the gun. She had found another more interesting toy. Searching for where it went, I turned and saw Olivia. She had come down from the swing and was holding it between her small hands.

"No, Olivia, no," I said, but it was too late.

Olivia fired the gun.

The bullet hissed through the air and hit Mary Ellen in the chest, and she screamed and fell into the grass. I ran to Olivia, took the gun from between her hands, and then took her in my arms, sobbing.

"Oh, sweetie. Oh, baby."

I grabbed Christine as well and held them both so tight I wasn't sure I'd ever let them go. Meanwhile, the officers attended to Mary Ellen, and I heard them call for an ambulance.

"Did I kill her?" Olivia asked, terrified.

I looked at Mary Ellen. She was still moving. I shook my head. "Oh, no, baby. She's not dead."

"She was being so mean to you, Mommy."

I hugged her again and kissed her forehead. "I know, sweetie. I know."

"I want to go home now, Mommy."

I nodded. "Let's do that."

I lifted Christine in my arms, then grabbed Olivia's hand in mine. I walked with them past Mary Ellen on the ground. She was wailing in pain. In the distance, I heard more sirens approach and knew it had to be the ambulance. I held my kids very tight all the way to the car, then took off down the street, promising the sergeant in charge that I would give them my full report the very next day, but now, I just wanted to go home. For once, I couldn't wait to walk through my front door.

# Epilogue
## TWO WEEKS LATER

I walked into the living room and spotted Chad on the couch, watching some cooking show on TV. I had tucked both girls in, and they were heavily asleep already. They had just had their first day at their new preschool, where they assured me no one would ever be able to pick them up without having permission to do so.

I sat next to him, then leaned on his shoulder. He pushed me away. I tried to kiss him, but he moved his face. I sighed.

"Are you seriously still angry with me?" I said. "You've barely said a word for two weeks."

"Well, can you blame me for being angry?" he asked, finally looking at me. "You almost got our kids killed!"

I exhaled. "I'm trying here, okay?"

"I just... I can't believe you. You lie to me so that you can go to work? Is work really that important to you? More important than the girls and me? Than your own family? Because once we start lying to one another, then...."

"I know. I know. It's like cancer for the marriage. I do see that it was wrong of me. I just thought that... well, I messed up, okay?"

Chad's eyes eased up. He nodded. "Okay. I just... I don't get why work is so important to you."

"I get that it can be hard to understand," I said. "But I think I realized through this case that I might be trying to somehow make up for what happened to my sister.

Some days, I think that's why I became an FBI agent—because I couldn't save Sydney. In many ways, I think I have tried to make up for it ever since because of all the guilt I feel. I keep wondering why he chose her and not me. We don't know if she is even alive anymore. Probably not."

Chad exhaled and crossed his hands in front of his chest. "I'm not sure that makes much sense to me. But I haven't tried being in your shoes. I can't stop thinking about our future and if this is how it's going to be. Are you not going to prioritize us anymore?"

"Are you afraid I'm gonna neglect you, Chad Wilson?" I asked with a light laugh.

He smirked. "Well… yeah. I guess I am. Is that bad?"

"A little bit, but I get it."

He leaned back on the couch. I reached over and pulled his lips against mine. This time, he didn't pull away.

"How about I make it up to you?" I asked between kisses.

"And just how do you plan to do that?"

"Well, how about I give you what you want most of all?"

His eyes lit up, and a smile spread across his face.

"You don't mean…?"

I nodded. "Yes, my love. Let's make another child."

He leaned forward and pushed me down on the couch, then kissed my neck.

"Just make sure it's a boy this time," he said, laughing.

"Or what?" I asked when he pulled my shirt off.

He kissed me again and pushed me down.

"Or we'll just have to keep trying till we succeed."

"I was thinking maybe we could call him Alex."

He stopped. "Alex? Hmm, I kind of like that. Where did that come from?"

I smiled gently. "I've always liked that name."

. . .

**THE END**

THIS STORY CONTINUES in the first book in The Eva Rae Thomas Mystery Series, ***DON'T LIE TO ME.***

You can get the mystery novel in bookstores or online at Amazon, Barnes and Noble, Walmart, and many other places.

# Afterword

Dear Reader,

Thank you for purchasing **So We Lie.** I hope you enjoyed reading it as much as I enjoyed writing it.

This novel is a prequel to my entire Eva Rae Thomas series. It was fun meeting Eva Rae as her younger and ambitious self, digging into those emotions, and exploring what went wrong in her marriage.

I have a feeling this Alexander Huxley guy will play a more prominent role later in her life as well.

The idea to write this book came to me because one of my good friends started to date a guy she had met online and who lived in Italy.

He is now in the U.S., and they live together, and he seems like a very nice guy.

But, of course, I kept thinking about what could go wrong in a relationship like that and started to read about the scams, and that's how I heard about the trafficking stories similar to this one, and I thought that was absolutely awful.

So, naturally, I had to put it in a book.

The idea for this trafficking story is a mix of events I have read that have actually taken place, which terrified me greatly.

Every month I support an organization: I AM A FREEDOM FIGHTER. Their goal is to end ALL human trafficking. You can read more about them here: https://www.iamafreedomfighter.org

Thank you for all your support, and remember to leave a review if you can. It's greatly appreciated.

Take care,

Willow

## About the Author

Willow Rose is a multi-million-copy best-selling Author and an Amazon ALL-star Author of more than 80 novels.

Several of her books have reached the top 10 of ALL books on Amazon in the US, UK, and Canada. She has sold more than three million books all over the world.

She writes Mystery, Thriller, Paranormal, Romance, Suspense, Horror, Supernatural thrillers, and Fantasy.

Willow's books are fast-paced, nail-biting, page-turners with twists you won't see coming. That's why her fans call her The Queen of Scream.

Willow lives on Florida's Space Coast with her husband and two daughters. When she is not writing or reading, you will find her surfing and watch the dolphins play in the waves of the Atlantic Ocean.

To be the first to hear about new releases and bargains—from Willow Rose—sign up below to be on the VIP List. (I promise not to share your email with anyone else, and I won't clutter your inbox.)

---

**Win a waterproof Kindle e-reader or a $125 Amazon giftcard**!
Just become a member of my Facebook group **WILLOW ROSE - MYSTERY SERIES**.
Every time we pass 1000 new members, we'll randomly select a winner from all the entries.

To enter, just tap/click here:
https://www.facebook.com/groups/1921072668197253

---

**Tired of too many emails?** Text the word: "willowrose" to 31996 to sign up to Willow's VIP text List to get a text alert with news about New Releases, Giveaways, Bargains and Free books from Willow.

Follow Willow on BookBub

*Connect with Willow online:*
https://www.facebook.com/willowredrose
https://twitter.com/madamwillowrose
http://www.goodreads.com/author/show/4804769.Willow_Rose
https://www.willow-rose.net
Mail to: contact@willow-rose.net

To be the first to hear about **exclusive new releases and FREE ebooks from Willow Rose**, sign up below to be on the VIP List. (I promise not to share your email with anyone else, and I won't clutter your inbox.)

- GO HERE TO SIGN UP TO BE ON THE VIP LIST :
http://readerlinks.com/l/415254
Or scan this QR code with your phone:

**Tired of too many emails?** Text the word: "willowrose" to 31996 to sign up to Willow's VIP text List to get a text alert with news about New Releases, Giveaways, Bargains and Free books from Willow.

---

FOLLOW WILLOW ROSE ON BOOKBUB:
https://www.bookbub.com/authors/willow-rose